ONE HUNDRED WISHES

KELLY COLLINS

KELLY COLLINS
The Queen of Hearts

Cover photograph by Darren Birks Photography

Cover design by Victoria Cooper Art

To my family. I hope your wishes come true.

CHAPTER ONE

Samantha White looked into the mirror but no longer recognized herself. She'd come a long way from the girl who lived in the back seat of her mother's car. With blue hair and a five-thousand-dollar leather jacket, she hardly knew the woman staring back at her.

"Indigo, you're on in five," Brenda, the assistant to her assistant called from the door.

She looked into the mirror. "You can do this," she said to the scared girl who lived inside her. The young woman she'd buried under hair dye and designer clothes. "You *have* to do this." She pulled her ID card and a wad of cash from her purse and shoved it inside her back pocket. "I *will* do this," she said to herself as she walked toward the stage.

At the edge of the curtain stood her agent, Oliver Shepherd, and her manager, Dave Belton. One handled her career, the other handled her life. She was tired of being handled—*man*handled.

"You ready?" Dave gripped her arms too tightly. She hated it when he was pumped up on something. She wouldn't call him abusive in her opinion. She'd seen what abuse looked like firsthand when her drunken father beat her mother nearly to death. No, Dave was a control freak and a cocaine freak—not a good mix when the star of your show wasn't keen on continuing to be an indentured servant. That's why Oliver Shepherd was here tonight in Denver. He was present to secure their futures.

"Don't forget the playlist. None of that slow, lover's-lament shit you want to sing lately. No one wants to hear sad stuff. These are hard times, and people look to you to lift them up." He turned her around and gave her a push toward the stage.

"Knock 'em dead, Indigo," Oliver said. "We'll meet up at the hotel to sign the new deal."

She smiled on the outside and put on her headset. Her hand reached to her back pocket to confirm the presence of phase one of her escape plan, a plan that took her years to put into place. There was no walking away from the power of the Shepherd Agency or the grip of Dave Belton.

It wasn't an easy decision to run away from her life when so many people depended on her, but Samantha knew she'd never survive another year like the past one. Thirty-six countries and two hundred and ten concerts in fifty-two weeks. Add two new albums and three music awards, and she was done. While her alter ego Indigo was a powerhouse, Samantha White was burned out.

The sold-out venue hummed with the deafening chant of "In-di-go, In-di-go, In-di-go."

Her heart raced. The rush of blood to her head dizzied her. The minute she walked on stage, she earned five hundred and sixty thousand dollars, but it wasn't enough. There wasn't an amount large enough to keep her in the spotlight. There were at least three things Samantha wanted more than money.

She wanted a life.

She wanted to love.

She wanted the freedom that came from being invisible.

She'd get none of those things living under the microscope of fame or the strong arm of her manager.

She was America's sweetheart. At twenty-nine, she still looked sixteen, which was a curse because the public's perception was everything when you were famous. She wanted to act her age, but having a glass of wine or a date went against her squeaky-clean brand.

Her real life wasn't too far off from the lie they told the public. She drank, but she did it alone in her hotel room or on her bus. She dated, but only in secret, and she was limited to band members and stage hands. When she complained, Dave offered her his magic elixir —a concoction of drugs and alcohol he guaranteed would cheer her up. She knew then it was time to go. She didn't want to be another Amy Winehouse or Janis Joplin.

When the drummer started the distinctive beat of her last platinum single, "Your Way" she walked out onto the stage for what she hoped would be her last contractual live performance.

For an hour and forty-six minutes, she gave the audience everything she had. For her final song, she walked to the band and told them what she wanted to sing. They gave her that look, the one that said Dave would be furious, but if she was going to walk away, it would be on her terms.

Gary, her lead guitarist, counted off the beats to start the song "Empty Box". She glanced over her shoulder to stage right, to the red-faced Dave flailing his hands in the air. Behind him, Oliver Shepherd frowned. It wasn't what they wanted, but it was what she wanted. After ten years of contract slavery, wasn't it time she got her way?

She belted out the song about a life not lived, and on the chorus she walked down the steps and disappeared into the crowd.

The fans swarmed around her as she pushed her way toward the back of the arena.

"Ohmigod, Ohmigod, Ohmigod!" a blue-haired teenage girl, dressed in jeans and a gray hoodie screamed. "It's you! It's really you!"

Samantha smiled. "It's *almost* me." She pointed to the girl's hoodie and then back to her studded leather jacket. "Want to trade?" Samantha heard the security team closing in, telling people to, "Move aside." She had minutes to make her escape.

"You want to trade with me? Ohmigod, Ohmigod, Ohmigod! Yes!" The teen stripped her jacket off like it was on fire and traded it for Indigo's custom-designed look. While the girl stood putting her new fashion-forward coat on, Indigo pulled the hoodie over her blue hair and blended in with the crowd.

She felt bad for the girl who would soon be accosted by her security team in seconds and whisked away to the back room. Eventually, they'd figure out she wasn't Indigo, but a super fan who had the perfect shade of blue hair and the same physique. She couldn't feel too badly because whoever the girl was, she'd get her fifteen minutes of fame and a rockin' hot custom leather jacket.

At the front of the arena with Indigo left behind, Samantha White flagged down a cab and gave him the address to the second phase of her plan. He drove her to the airport, where a used front-wheel drive was parked in space number nine-three-seven.

She tipped the cabbie and watched him drive away. Inside the front right wheel well, she felt for the keys her assistant Deanna promised would be there. They fell off the tire and into her palm. She opened the door, sank into the driver's seat and sent a silent thanks to her assistant and only real friend. Deanna had watched Samantha wither under the constant stress and abuse. She'll never forget the day they sat down and planned Samantha's escape. She'd be forever grateful for her loyalty and help.

It took over two years because she needed to fulfill her public engagements or face multiple lawsuits. She couldn't believe she'd made it out alive and mostly well.

Samantha was young and naïve when Oliver Shepherd discovered her singing in a honky-tonk bar in Nashville. He saw what she didn't. She had star power, and he took advantage of her by offering her a ten-year deal. She thought he was being generous, but in reality, he was hedging a sure bet and locking down his talent.

While Samantha thought how freeing a steady paycheck could be for her and her mom, the management team added up the millions she would make them.

She bought her mom a house and gave her the life she'd always wanted. Samantha continued to dream about her life ahead. While her mother enjoyed the fruits of her daughter's labor, Samantha was a workhorse who didn't get a second to breathe.

She couldn't complain about her life too much because she'd been the one to sign her name on the dotted line. She was slow to investigate and quick to act.

One bright note was her management team was fair with compensation, but they were relentless when it came to work ethic. They would get their pound of flesh from her one way or another. At five-foot-five and down to a hundred and four pounds, she had no more flesh to offer.

She glanced around the car. The back seat was filled with suitcases of clothes. The front seat held a bag with more cash than the car was worth. It was risky to leave it all out here in a parking lot, but what price could she put on survival? She opened the cooler on the floor and found her favorite drink, a sugar-free, calorie-free lemonade that tasted almost as good as the real thing. For the next five minutes, Samantha White sat in silence and enjoyed freedom and anonymity. In the glove compartment was a knit cap, along with a pair of sunglasses she wouldn't need until tomorrow.

She pulled off the hoodie and stuffed her sapphire locks into the hat. She laughed at how they'd come up with her name and brand. No wonder she was blue.

"You can't be Samantha White. It's a boring name," Oliver said. "Let me see your eyes."

She lifted her face into the light. Her mom always said her eyes were blue, while drunken Daddy said they were black as tar, like her soul. Then again, he didn't see straight after having a fifth of hard liquor for breakfast.

"Indigo," Dave said. "Her eyes are a black-blue." By that time, Dave was hired to be her manager—really a babysitter because she had recently turned nineteen. Not old enough to know better, but old enough to make legal decisions. It made her dangerous in their eyes.

Once they'd named her "Indigo," her future was set. She'd adopted a persona with blue hair, edgy clothes, and a squeaky-clean image. It was the dichotomy of her appearance versus her persona that drew attention. She was every parent's nightmare and dream in the same girl. Throw in a voice with a range to rival Whitney Houston, and she was a hit. All she had to do was show up. That was where Dave Belton came in.

Dave's superpower was his ability to instill fear. He scared the hell out of her. After the first time she mouthed off at him and found herself locked inside her hotel room, she rarely gave him trouble. He reminded her of her father. If he could hold her hostage, he was capable of anything.

Mixing attitude with alcohol made the impossible possible. She'd learned that lesson the hard way. She thought of the time her father put her mother into the hospital. Yvette White was unconscious for three days. After she was released, she packed her and Samantha's belongings and moved from place to place, never staying anyplace long enough for Harlan White to find them. Funny how life had come full circle; now she had packed up her stuff and was hiding again.

"Welcome to your life, Samantha." It was odd to hear her real name, even from her own voice. Everyone called her Indigo, even her mother. She turned on the dome light and pulled down the visor to inspect herself in the mirror. "You're almost you." She plucked the false lashes from her eyes and flicked them out the window. That was her past. This was her beginning.

"Aspen Cove, here I come."

She took an hour to get used to driving. Although she maintained a driver's license, she rarely got behind the wheel. The last time she went out for a drive, she was swarmed by paparazzi and had to call her security team to come and get her. She loved the fans, but there was something to be said for freedom.

Before she entered the mountain pass, she pulled into a fast-food drive-thru. It was her first test at being invisible. She checked herself in the mirror and tucked the remaining strands of blue away.

"Welcome, what can I get you?" said the young female voice through the speaker.

"One second, please." Samantha couldn't remember a time when she'd sat in a drive-thru looking over the menu. Her food was portioned, calorie-counted, and delivered. She'd spent the first year starving and the next nine pretending food was poison. It made it easier to not eat. Now a menu of burgers and fries were staring at her. She was the proverbial kid in a candy shop. "I'm ready."

"Me too," the girl called back.

"I'll have a cheeseburger and fries and a chocolate shake. Oh, and can I have a box of those animal cookies, and maybe some apple slices?" She didn't know if she'd get to the apple slices, but she ordered them because it at least made the meal seem balanced.

The girl gave her a total and told her to drive around.

Samantha held her breath when the window opened and the teenager looked at her. For a second she thought she'd been recognized, then the girl said, "I have the same cap."

"Cool." Samantha handed over a twenty and took her food. She was on a roll. She pulled into the parking spot reserved for to-go orders and texted Deanna.

Operation Indi-go-go is a success. She shot a picture of her food and laughed.

Dave would have an aneurysm if he saw what you are eating, she wrote back. **I'm glad you're safe. Everything is taken care of. The key is under the mat. The furniture is in place. The place is basic, but the view is nice. You'll need lots of stuff once you get settled. I found a cool headboard at a consignment shop in town. It was closed for the season, but when I said I had cash, some lady named Abby was happy to open for me. You'll love it.**

She pulled the phone to her chest and hugged it.

I appreciate everything you've done.

Deanna took a vacation and traveled to Aspen Cove to accept a delivery of basic furniture and a bed before she started her real vacation hundreds of miles away in Alaska.

You might not thank me when you don't have coffee in the morning, but there's a diner in town and the food is decent. Now turn off your phone or they'll track it. Enjoy what time you get. Hugs.

Samantha powered down her phone and headed for Aspen Cove. She turned on the eighties station and sang to the old-school music she loved while she had her first burger and fries in years. She knew this wasn't a permanent vacation. She still had commitments left to fulfill. Her last real planned public event was important. Although her management team was pissed off she was doing it for free, the event was for victims of domestic abuse, and she was excited to help. She had a final album due for the record label, but at least she'd get downtime until they found her. They *would* find her. That was a certainty. Between now and then, she'd need to come up with a plan B.

Nearly three hours later, she pulled into the tiny town of Aspen Cove. Everything was dark except the diner where a group of people seemed to be celebrating. If it weren't so late and she weren't so tired, she'd consider crashing their party. She had a lot to celebrate, too.

She pulled into the driveway of 7 Lake Circle and took in a deep breath. This was it. She danced her way to the front door. Under the mat, like Deanna said, was the key. She slid it into the lock and opened the door to a whole different world.

CHAPTER TWO

"Can I have everyone's attention?" Dalton Black stood in the center of Maisey's Diner and let out a whistle that could be heard across the lake. "We're here to celebrate a lot of things." He picked up the glass of wine in front of him. "First, I want to thank Cannon and Bowie for supplying the alcohol."

The raucous group yipped and hollered. Everyone loved free booze.

"Second, I wanted to say I love you to my mom, who made this diner possible along with the help and support of Doc Parker and the community." He shuddered to think where their lives would be if the people of Aspen Cove hadn't protected and cared for them. That was the best thing about living here. Everyone was family.

When Dalton was a teen and his mom was beaten and bruised, Doc Parker offered up the building for their future. Although her outer shell had recovered, Dalton knew even as a teen the internal scars from years of abuse would take the longest to heal.

Despite it all, Maisey Black moved forward. She'd made the diner a success and paid back the note owed to Doc in record time.

Maisey's Diner belonged to his mom, though she insisted he was a full partner.

"I want to welcome my new brothers, Cannon and Bowie, to my family. I want to give my new dad a hug." He pulled Ben Bishop to his side and gave him a squeeze. If Ben, who spent years drunk and pining for his dead wife could turn himself around and make Maisey Black fall in love with him, anything was possible.

"In a matter of moments, I went from being an only child to one of three sons." He looked at Bowie and Cannon, his new stepbrothers and longtime friends. Next to Bowie stood his wife Katie cradling their newborn daughter Sahara. "I also became an uncle." He found Cannon in the crowd and gave him a knowing look. "I have one more thing to say, and then I'm done." He glanced between the two sets of newlyweds in the room, Ben and Maisey and Bowie and Katie. "Stop with this love shit. It's like a virus in this town, and I don't want to catch it." He lifted his glass and said, "Cheers!"

Dalton shook his head at his friends who were all laughing and enjoying a night of friendship and camaraderie.

Ben had carted his mom Maisey to Denver last week and married her at the county courthouse. He could have tied the knot here where Doc would have been happy to officiate, but Ben wanted it to be special, so he sprung for a weekend at the Brown Palace Hotel.

Dalton had never seen his mother so happy, but tonight was about something else altogether, and his part in the charade was to make it seem like it was Maisey and Ben's night to celebrate—again. Since they'd been celebrating every night since they returned, no one would be the wiser.

Cannon brought Sage to the center of the crowd. "I have a few things to say myself." He nodded to Dalton, which was his cue to get Sage's sister, Lydia, who'd been hiding in the kitchen for almost an hour. It was a good thing she was hungry when she arrived because he didn't know what to do with the woman besides feed her. Dalton had a soft spot for Sage, but her sister was a whole other beast. Never had he seen two people come from the same set of parents and be so different. Sage had flaming red hair, while her sister was blonde. Sage had green eyes, while her sister's were blue. Sage was no bigger than four stacked milk crates, while Lydia came to his chin, which meant she had to be five-foot-six or seven. Sage was always happy, but her sister spent most of her time crying over pie. Dalton didn't do well with teary-eyed women.

He snuck into the kitchen and said, "It's time." Lydia scooped another bite of Maisey's famous cherry pie into her mouth and followed him out.

As soon as Cannon saw Lydia, he dropped to a knee in front of Sage. She looked at him like he'd had a stroke and fell to her knees in front of him.

"You okay? Are you sick? Too much wine?" She lifted her hand to his head and felt him for fever. The nurse in her never took a break.

He laughed. "I am sick, and I'll never recover," he said with dramatic flair. "I caught the bug Dalton talked about."

She tilted her head the way her three-legged dog Otis did when he was confused. Then she looked behind Cannon to see her sister. Sage jumped to her feet and ran past him to Lydia. Poor Cannon might never get those four words he wanted to ask out.

Sage threw her arms around Lydia's neck. "You're here." She stepped back with a look of concern. "What are you doing here? Are you okay?"

Dalton thought it was funny how everything around him had changed so fast. How his two friends who were sworn bachelors had fallen hard and fast.

When Sage and Katie arrived in town, nothing stayed the same.

He looked across the darkened street to Bea's bakery and thought about the old woman responsible for this love fest. How her gifts of the bed and breakfast to Sage and the bakery to Katie brought the town together. Her act of selflessness had healed so many hurts.

Lydia wiped the tears from her eyes. "I'm fine. I'm here because..." She nodded her head toward Cannon, who was still on one knee but facing no one. "Go to your man, he has something to ask you." Lydia widened her eyes and made a face.

"Oh my God." Sage looked at all the nodding heads and raced back to stand in front of Cannon. "I'm sorry. You have my full attention."

Cannon chuckled. "I'll take whatever piece of you I can get, even if it's your short attention span." He wiped his hands on his jeans and reached into his pocket to pull out a small white box, then he cleared his throat.

Dalton wasn't sure if Cannon was trying to gain his composure or get the attention of everyone in the room. Either way, all eyes were on him.

"Sage, I wanted to do this on Valentine's Day, but I heard it was a cliché. Then I wanted to do it last week on lucky St. Patrick's Day, but Dad beat me to it by marrying Maisey. So, today is it, sweetheart." He reached for her hand and held it to his heart. "I loved you the day I met you. Well, I hated you in my head, but I loved you in my heart."

The room erupted in laughter. Dalton hadn't been present that day, but rumor said they had a doozy of a first meeting.

Sage pulled back and looked down at him. "Cannon Bishop, if this is the way you're going to propose, I'll walk out of here with what's in the box, but you'll walk out with a black eye." She fisted her hands on her hips. "You can do better. Give me the best you've got."

Doc Parker walked up and placed his hand on Cannon's shoulder. "You're screwing this up, son." He looked at Sage. His white brows arched toward the ceiling. "The boy loves you. He wants to marry you. What do you say, young lady?"

"Thanks, Doc, I got this." Cannon turned back to Sage. "I do love you. I can't imagine a life without you. I want to marry you so I can love you forever." He opened the box to reveal a gold band imbedded with tiny diamonds. Cannon's attention drifted to Katie and then back to Sage. "A certain blonde baker told me a gold band was all you wanted, but it wasn't enough. You need a little sparkle in your life. Sage Nichols, will you marry me?"

Her sister Lydia burst into tears. Dalton wasn't sure if they were happy tears or sad tears. He was betting they were a little of both.

Sage dropped to her knees in front of Cannon and threw her arms around his neck, sending the box and ring flying into the air. Dalton caught it mid-flight and hoped it wasn't like catching the bouquet at a wedding. He needed a woman like he needed another six years in prison.

"You're the only sparkle I need, Cannon Bishop," Sage said. "Yes, I'll marry you."

Dalton tossed the box back to Cannon. "Get the ring on her finger before she comes to her senses and changes her mind."

Cannon slipped the band on Sage's finger. The crowd lifted their wine glasses to toast.

This time, it was Sheriff Cooper who had something to say. He pointed at all the Bishops in the house. There were six now that Katie, Maisey, and baby Sahara took the last name. "We're being taken over by Bishops." He looked to Bobby Williams, who stood in the corner with his wife Louise. "Dude, they're giving you a run for your money."

Bobby gave everyone a sly smile and placed his hand on his wife's stomach. "Number eight is cooking."

Doc Parker groaned. "We know what causes that."

After everyone closed their open mouths, the group went wild. If there was one thing the Williamses did well, it was breed. They had the cutest kids, but Dalton couldn't imagine having one child, nonetheless eight.

One more look at Bowie and Katie, and he erased the thought. Sahara was a miracle baby born to a mother with the biggest heart he knew. It was a donor heart of a woman he'd grown up with. Looking at Bowie, he knew the man was one lucky bastard to have fallen in love with the same heart twice. Dalton would be lucky to find love once. Who'd fall in love with a man like him?

Katie handed Sahara off to Bowie and picked up the cake she'd baked for the occasion. She brought it to Sage and Cannon. "I did it. I mastered high-altitude cake baking." She handed Sage the pan, then jumped up and down like she'd discovered the cure for cancer. "It's even—I didn't have to balance it out with extra frosting!"

Bowie came up behind his wife and pressed his lips to her cheek. "I loved my lopsided cake." Bowie's homecoming cake had an extra quart of frosting on one side to cover up Katie's baking inexperience.

"You loved me," Katie reminded.

Dalton groaned. "It's getting far too thick and sweet in here." He gave his new dad a test. "Hey, Pops," he called to Ben. "I'm outta here. Can you lock up when everyone is finished?"

"Sure thing, son," Ben replied.

Dalton walked toward the door with a smile on his face. It wasn't the life he'd envisioned for himself all those years ago, but it was *his* life, and somehow it seemed to work.

Sheriff Cooper caught up to him. "Keep your eyes open on the way home. I think the kids suspected of burning down the house across the lake are from Copper Creek. Arsonists rarely stop with one. If you see anything, don't act on it, call me."

Dalton gave him an I'm-not-an-idiot look. "It's all good. I'll call you if I see anything." He walked outside into the chill of the March night. The sky was clear, and a million stars guided him toward home.

The sheriff needn't worry. Dalton took no chances with his freedom these days. If he had a drink, he walked home or got a ride. If he saw a fight, he stepped aside. Six years in prison for killing someone was enough for him.

Although life seemed to throw him a lot of curve balls, family and friends remained a consistent source of comfort. He looked over his shoulder at the crowd he left at the diner. Those were the people who mattered most in his life.

As he walked the mile up Main Street to Lake Circle, he thought about his future. There would be no falling in love. No engagement. No wedding. No babies. Dalton's life was fine the way it was, he liked the status quo. He liked the peacefulness of living in a town where he wasn't judged. In Aspen Cove, he was safe and invisible.

He rounded the corner and walked to his back porch. There were lights on in the cabin next door. Odd because it had been vacant for over two years. There had been no mention of anyone moving in. Cannon told him he thought an investment banker bought it for future development. Dalton would have ignored the light in the window and walked inside his cabin if it weren't for the smoke billowing from under the back door.

CHAPTER THREE

She expected rustic, but Samantha never expected *Little House on the Prairie*. The place was cold, damp and dull. She pulled her knit cap tighter over her head and zipped up the hoodie all the way to her neck. She found the thermostat on the wall and cranked it to high, but nothing happened.

Several years of vacancy and neglect showed. There wasn't an ounce of homeyness to the cabin except for the flowers Deanna left on the new coffee table she had delivered.

It wasn't as if Samantha was used to homey since she spent most of her life in hotel rooms and tour buses, but she liked heat. Right now if she could get warm, she'd be happy to skip homey altogether.

Feeling the chill of the cold mountain air in her bones, she zeroed in on the fireplace already set up to burn with logs stacked in the opening and a few cones of newspaper peeking out between the chopped wood. On the mantel sat a box of wooden matches. *Thank you, Deanna.*

She hurried over and grabbed them hoping she could get a blaze started before she unpacked her car or froze to death. There was nothing worse than being exhausted except being cold and exhausted. Her stomach rumbled, and she experienced a new worst. Being tired, cold and hungry was a trifecta.

It took a dozen strikes of the match to get it lit. Her icy cold fingers shook as she held the flame to the newspaper. Pure joy raced through her as the tiny flicker turned into a flame and built into an inferno. Her joy was short-lived when rolling clouds of gray and black smoke filled the room.

Not knowing what to do, Samantha took the metal poker leaning against the stone fireplace and shifted the wood. Her thought was it needed to be pushed deeper into the opening, but the action caused a wall of black smoke to rush at her.

"Great, just great." She looked around the cabin, hoping for an answer to her problem. The only solution was to put the fire out and open the door. Her moment of success turned into a crushing defeat when she realized the only heat she'd feel was from the flames threatening to burn down her secret retreat.

Without further deliberation, she grabbed the vase on the table and poured the water and flowers onto the flames. The hiss and sizzle brought with it another burst of smoke that burned her throat and threatened to choke her.

Sorely in need of fresh air, she ran for the door. As she reached for the knob, the door swung open with force. The power behind it sent her flying across the room to land flat on her ass.

A hulk of a man raced inside. Samantha was certain he was a kidnapper, or worse, a murderer. If the angry look on his face was any sign of his intent, she'd go with a murderer.

"Who the hell are you?" Over six feet of solid muscle stalked toward her like a bobcat closing in on its prey.

She spider-crawled backward until the wall stopped her progress. She was good and trapped.

He loomed over her big and scary while he pulled out his phone and dialed a number.

She tried to stand up, but he gave her a look that flattened her back to the floor. "I live here," she whispered.

"Right." He narrowed his eyes and shook his head. "Coop. I'm at the vacant next to mine. I've got your arsonist."

There was a moment of silence.

"I'm no—"

Her words halted when he raised his hand.

"Some scrawny little boy. Can't be over sixteen." He pointed to her and mouthed the words "Stay," then stepped back and rubbed his beard. "I haven't touched him—yet." Steely blue eyes held her in place.

He ended the call and shoved his phone inside his pocket. "Sheriff's on his way."

"Good," she said. She sat up taller and pulled the cap from her head, letting her blue hair tumble across her shoulders. "I'm not a scrawny little boy, you idiot. I'm a full-grown woman. Who the hell are you?"

Though his eyes gave way to surprise, his voice didn't waver. "Neighborhood watch."

He gave her a black look while his eyes traveled up and down her body.

She could see why he thought she was a little boy. Dressed in jeans and an oversized hoodie, her shape was straight and boxy. When her long hair was tucked inside a gray cap, there was nothing about her that screamed woman.

"Girl? Maybe. Woman? Doubtful. Arsonist? Most likely."

Samantha pulled her knees to her chest and ran her fingers through her hair. "I'm not an arsonist. I own this cabin. I was trying to get warm."

He nodded. "Right. Tell your story to the sheriff." He backed his big body toward the door and leaned against the frame like a sentry on duty.

A breeze whipped through the room and wrapped around her like an icy cloak. Teeth chattering, she asked, "C-c-can you at least shut the d-d-door?"

He shoved his hands into his pockets. "Nope."

She saw the flashing lights reflect off the window. "Great. All I wanted was a warm place to camp out for a few weeks, and now my mug shot will be posted everywhere." She buried her head against her knees. "Perfect."

"You picked the wrong neighborhood—and the wrong neighbor."

Seconds later, a big man dressed in beige and brown entered the cabin. Mr. Neighborhood Watch nodded toward him. "Hey, Coop. This little waif said she was looking for a place to squat for a few weeks."

Samantha scrambled to her feet and pressed her body to the wooden wall. "I said no such thing."

"You can add liar to her list of infractions."

She wasn't sure if it was him or the cold that got her moving, but she knew one thing for certain. She was no longer freezing. In fact, she was hotter than a cinder. She'd been called many things, but liar wasn't one.

"My name is Samantha White, and I own this damn cabin." She stomped forward until the sheriff placed his hand on his pistol. Then she stopped dead still like road kill.

"I'm Sheriff Cooper, and you need to stay right there." The sheriff eased his hand from his weapon. "Do you have identification? Proof you are who you claim to be?"

Thankfully, Deanna was an efficient assistant. She'd had the utilities, homeowners insurance and cable put in Samantha's name. The papers were supposed to be in the top drawer in the kitchen. Besides those, she had a driver's license.

"Yes."

The sheriff looked at the other man. "Dalton, you got coffee at your place? I could use a cup."

No way. Samantha couldn't believe the big oaf standing by the door was Dalton. Could it be the same Dalton Black she remembered as a child? She'd spent the entire three months living in Aspen Cove staring at him. He was five years ahead of her in school, but so handsome. Something raw and vulnerable drew her in back then. There was nothing vulnerable about Dalton Black these days. He was a cross between cover model and serial killer.

She peeked around the sheriff to get a better look at Dalton the man. She could see it was the same person. Dark hair. Cold, steely eyes. Dark, brooding personality. He was at least a foot taller and a foot wider, but the scar that floated over his brow was still there. Covered by his beard, she could imagine the cleft in his chin also remained.

Before she could say anything, Dalton was out the door and down the steps. Gone.

"You say your name is Samantha White?"

"I am Samantha White."

The sheriff gave her a full head-to-toe inspection. She knew he was calculating the risks. Would she run? Would she do something worse? She'd watched enough *CSI* in hotel rooms to know he'd started his investigative profiling of her the minute he arrived. Looking like an out-of-control teen wouldn't help her case.

"All right, Samantha White with the blue hair, show me your identification?"

She pointed to the bag on the table. The only thing she'd brought into the cabin. In it was a stash of cash and her ID. The cash would make her look guilty of something, but her ID could at least prove she was telling the truth. "You want me to get it, or do you want to get it?" She didn't want her first taste of freedom to end in death.

He looked at the small duffel bag. "You can get it. Just move slowly."

Relief flooded through her. She didn't want to have to explain the thousands of dollars she had in cash, but when she opened the bag, she realized she'd have to wade through the bricks of twenties to get to her driver's license at the bottom.

The sheriff stood over her. When she dared to glance at him, his left brow nearly hit his hair.

She shoved the money to the side while she fished around. "I don't believe in credit cards, and having cash isn't illegal." She rummaged through the bag until she came up with the wallet where Deanna had stored her documents. "Here." She pulled out her driver's license and passed it to the sheriff's opened palm. "I'd offer you something to eat or drink, but I just arrived. I'm not set up for company."

He nodded toward the sofa still covered in protective plastic. "Have a seat."

She sat at the edge, the plastic crinkling under her as she took up the corner and once again pulled her knees to her chest. At least when Dalton left, he shut the door. The room wasn't warm, but there was no longer an icy breeze blanketing her. She glanced at the fireplace where sooty water leaked from inside. Her once pretty flowers lay wilted on top of charred wood. Not exactly how she envisioned her first night in town.

Sheriff Cooper pulled out his phone and dialed. In the silence, she heard a male voice on the other end. "Run this number for me," the sheriff said. He recited the numbers written on her California driver's license.

She made a mental note to give Deanna a bonus. She'd insisted Samantha keep her license up to date although she drove nowhere. She could hardly leave her house on her own. There were too many fans wanting an autograph, a picture, or any piece of her. That's why she came to Aspen Cove—to preserve the pieces she had left.

She remembered the townspeople as being friendly. A small town where everyone knew each other, but no one paid much attention. That was the impression from a glassy-eyed twelve-year-old girl, but she'd been wrong. It would appear Dalton Black paid attention to everything.

"So Samantha, what brings you to Aspen Cove?" He walked around the living room taking note of the new furniture. In front of the couch sat a coffee table that still had protective cardboard on the corners. He brushed his fingers across the mantel, but there was no dust.

"I needed a break—a vacation. I bought this house several years ago, but things have been crazy in my life."

He stared at her blue hair like she was going through a phase. "You say you bought the place a few years ago?"

She let her legs down and inched toward the edge of the sofa. Beneath the plastic, she could see it was a pretty cognac-colored leather. She wondered if she'd get to see the true warmth of the material or if she'd be spending her first night of freedom inside a jail cell. "If you let me, I can get you some proof I belong here."

The sheriff stood taller. "I'd love to see it."

She looked at the gun in his holster. "Promise not to shoot me?"

He chuckled. "I make no promises. Don't give me a reason to pull the trigger."

Her eyes went to the kitchen behind him. "I'm going to the kitchen where I have documents that will help."

He followed her to the small galley kitchen.

She held her breath when she opened the first drawer and let it out when she found a blue folder with everything she needed inside. In the left-hand pocket was a copy of her purchase agreement.

As soon as this was cleared up, Deanna was getting a hefty raise. Samantha handed over the documents and leaned against the old yellowed Formica counter. While the sheriff looked through the papers, she glanced around the kitchen. It didn't even have a microwave.

The stove was gas, which she liked. It was an old four burner like the one they had when she and Mom lived in the house on Gladiola Lane. That house was a dump, but she loved it because it meant she was no longer living in the old Toyota.

The sheriff's phone rang. He had a brief conversation with the man on the other end. "She is. Okay. That's great, Mark." He turned to Samantha and smiled. "Why Aspen Cove?" he asked as he folded the papers and slid them into the folder.

"I lived here as a kid."

"Welcome back." He pushed off the counter and walked toward

the door. He opened it to reveal Dalton coming up the stairs with two cups of steaming coffee. "She owns the place." Sheriff Cooper breezed past Dalton. "Give her my cup of coffee and teach her how to start a fire." The sheriff trotted down the steps and disappeared into the night.

CHAPTER FOUR

Nothing shocked him more than the sheriff's comment. The woman owned the house. Dalton didn't know if he should be relieved or worried. He'd accused his new neighbor of being an arsonist. Not too neighborly.

He stood at the threshold of the door with two cups of steaming coffee. "It looks like I owe you an apology." He eyed the mess in the fireplace. "I'm told a lesson in lighting a fire is in order."

She wrapped her arms around her body and tried to stop her teeth from chattering. If their positions were reversed, he would have slammed the door and walked away, leaving her on the porch, but she didn't. She looked longingly at the steaming coffee mugs and glanced at the mess in her fireplace.

In a small voice, she said, "I could use the coffee and a fire."

He gave her a half smile. "I'm sorry." He stepped inside and kicked the door shut with his foot. "A house on the other side of the lake burned to the ground last week. It's under investigation for arson. When I saw the smoke ..." He shrugged. "I'm sorry."

"Nice to know you pay attention." She reached for a cup and

held it cradled in her hands. Raising it to her mouth, she didn't take a drink. She breathed in the steam to warm her.

His chest tightened when he saw her fingertips were blue. "Lord, let's get you warm." He led her to the couch and tore open the plastic covering. He yanked and tugged until it came loose. "I'm assuming you wanted that gone."

She climbed into the far corner and leaned against the soft leather of the armrest. "You assume a lot of things, but yes, it needed to go."

He hated that her first impression of him would be that of an unreasonable man. He'd never been so quick to judge, but he'd learned from example. He hated how going to prison had changed him. He wanted to see the best in people, but he was a realist. Most people weren't that good.

Her body shook from the chill, but it was no wonder. She was as thin as a piece of dental floss. If not for that blue hair, she'd be easy to miss. Turn her sideways, and she'd all but disappear.

Funny how only minutes before he wanted to throttle her, and now his instinct to care and protect kicked in. He wanted to feed her, and fast, but first things were first. She needed to get warm. He unzipped his jacket and wrapped it around her. "This should keep you warm until I get the fire going."

She set the coffee down and snugged his jacket beneath her chin. "The fireplace won't work. Something's wrong with it. I had a nice blaze going until the whole room filled with smoke." She looked toward the muddy mess on her floor. "It's a miracle I didn't burn the place down."

Dalton laughed. "Good thing you didn't burn it down because then you would have proven me right. You would have been an arsonist."

"A homeless arsonist."

"I'll be right back." He dashed out the door and returned minutes later with a broom, a metal dustpan and an old metal trash bin. He made quick work of cleaning up the sodden mess that had been her fire. The wilted flowers lay on top of the debris.

"You have something against flowers?"

Her lips quirked into a smile. "No. I love them. I have something against burning my place down. The vase was filled with water, the flowers were a sacrifice."

Minutes later, he'd stacked new wood, shoved in bits of kindling and paper, and pointed to a metal handle inside the opening.

"The flue was closed. You need to make sure it's open, and the air is circulating, otherwise, you get a back draft and a lot of smoke."

He loved the way her cheeks blushed. "I've heard of a flue." She leaned forward and picked up the coffee. One sip had her face twisting.

"Too strong?"

"Elixir of the gods. Super hot, but I appreciate it."

"You could cool it down with cream, sweeten it with sugar." He looked past her to the kitchen. "Do you have any?"

She shook her head and took another sip. This time, she smiled and her expression turned soft.

"I have little in the way of provisions." She tucked her legs close to her body. She nearly disappeared under his jacket.

"You got furniture." He found the matches sitting on the coffee table and pulled a single stick out. "How did you sneak that past me?"

She shrugged. "My ass—, I mean, my friend took care of it."

"I've got a few friends I'd call asses too. Nice that he or she could get things moved in here for you."

There was that smile again. "It's a she, and her name is Deanna."

Something about that pleased him. He wouldn't have been surprised if it had been a he. On closer inspection, Samantha was a pretty woman. Pretty women didn't stay single for long.

He struck the match and started the kindling on fire. He watched as the heated air moved upward and out through the now open flue. One look at her wood supply, and he knew she'd be out soon. "This isn't going to last long. I'll bring over enough wood to get through a day or so. You'll want to call Zachariah Thomas. He can hook you up with wood and moonshine. Both of which will get you warm."

She laughed. "I'll stick with the wood. I can pay you for what you give me."

"Unnecessary, but call Zachariah soon. The days may be warming up, but the nights are always cold."

"Is that the same old man that lives up in the mountains?" She leaned forward to put her cup on the table. "He's still making shine?"

"You've heard of him?" Dalton took another good look at her. He didn't recognize her. He'd never known a person with blue hair, but even if he mentally ignored her colored head, she didn't seem familiar. "How is it you came to Aspen Cove?"

She pulled her upper lip between her teeth. She looked at him as if testing to see how trustworthy he was. As if she would divulge a big secret. When her lip popped free, she said, "I lived here seventeen years ago."

"No way. I would know you."

"You know everyone who's lived here?" She giggled. It was a sound that vibrated through his rigid walls and settled inside his chest.

Except for the time he spent in prison, he could say yes without a second thought. He knew everyone. If she were here seventeen years ago, he would have been seventeen. He should know her.

Now that the fire was burning well, he placed the metal screen in front and came to join her on the couch. He sat at the opposite end and stared in her direction.

He expected something to come to him, some glimmer of recognition, but nothing did. "You don't look familiar, but then again, I'm pretty sure you didn't have blue hair back then. How old were you seventeen years ago?" An hour ago he wouldn't have given her over sixteen, but now he could see she held herself like an adult. She was well-spoken and reserved. When she smiled, faint creases showed in the corners of her eyes. A sign of maturity, his mom told him when he asked her what crow's feet were.

"I was invisible. I was twelve, and I rode the school bus to Copper Creek with you."

He envisioned the forty-five minute bus ride and pressed his memory for familiar faces. He'd hated that bus, but it was the most economical way to get to school. Economics were important when being raised by a single parent. Money was tight.

His dad had recently passed away. Although the town was supportive, not one person would miss the bastard. The logging company said it was a freak accident, but Dalton was certain someone got tired of his father's bullying and felled him and a tree at the same time. Thankfully, the small life insurance policy buried the asshole and left a little extra to get Maisey's Diner open.

He searched his memory again and came up with a little girl with brown hair and eyes the color of a starless sky. "I remember you. You sat in the second row on the right and stared toward the back of the bus every day."

"That was me," she said, sounding pleased that he'd remembered. "I stared at you and wondered how long it would take for me to become one of the cool kids."

That was a lifetime ago. "I was never one of the cool kids."

She peeled his jacket from her body and rose to stand in front of the fire. "You were to me."

"So that makes you what?" He calculated the years. "Wow, you're like twenty-nine now." Time had been kind to her.

She nodded slowly. "Yep. That's a far cry from the sixteen you gave me earlier." She turned toward the fire and rubbed her hands close to the flames.

Her sweatshirt lifted to her hips when she bent over. Dalton laughed inside. Had he seen her ass the first time, he would have never confused her with a boy. She was definitely thin, but every muscle of her lean body was solid. He was certain he could bounce a quarter off that ass. It was round and firm and would fill his palms nicely.

He shook that thought from his mind. Generally, women were

nothing but trouble for him. He had too much going on in his life. He didn't need other distractions. He'd be neighborly, but he wasn't getting involved with Samantha White.

"What are your plans?" The longer she was here, the harder it would be for him to keep his distance. He couldn't take his eyes off her backside and how those jeans hugged every tiny curve she had.

"I'm not sure yet. I don't have a solid plan. Eventually, I'll have to go back to work, but I'm here now."

"Cannon said a broker made the purchase of this property. He thought it was an investor waiting to scoop up a piece of land here and there until they had enough to put a resort on the lake."

Her eyes opened wide. "Lord no, that would be a shame. It was purchased under my company's name, but it's for personal use."

Her company? That meant the little quiet girl from Aspen Cove did all right for herself. Dalton loved it when he heard stories of rags to riches. Not that buying a house in Aspen Cove made her rich by any means, but if she could afford a vacation home, she was doing better than most. "What do you do?"

She turned toward him. Her lower lip sank between her teeth. When it popped free, she said, "I'm in public relations. A small company called Ignite."

One look at the fire had him laughing. "I sure hope you do a better job igniting your clients' businesses than you do a fire."

She moved directly in front of the fire and backed herself against the screen. "We do okay. What about you?"

Dalton expected her to erupt into flames at any minute. He wasn't sure how much to tell her. It wasn't like she'd be a long-term resident. He believed in honesty. He had integrity. He wouldn't lie to her, but he wouldn't provide more truth than she asked for or needed.

"I studied culinary arts." That was true. He'd attended Escoffier in Denver before he went to prison.

"So, you're a chef. Lucky me—you cook food, and I eat it!" She came back to the couch and sat in the corner.

Now that he knew she wasn't an arsonist, he liked her. She was easy to be around. He'd accosted her in her own home, and here he sat on her couch, drinking coffee and talking about careers.

"I'll make you something before you leave to go back to where it is you live full-time."

"That sounds great. Who knows, I could live here full-time if the food is good."

He let his eyes travel over her body. "I have a feeling you don't eat much." He rose from the couch. "Is there anything else you need? Any other crimes I can accuse you of? Any more insults I can toss your way before I leave?"

She rolled to her feet and walked to the front door to open it. Shivering when the cold wind whipped inside, she said, "I think I've been sufficiently humbled for the day. Thank you."

"Perfect. Glad I could help." He stepped outside and rubbed his arms. The T-shirt was poor protection from the biting cold.

"Oh my God, I almost stole your coat. I can't imagine the sheriff wanting to make another trip for a petty crime." She rushed to the couch where his coat lay and picked it up. She brought it to her nose and inhaled. "You smell nice."

He didn't think he'd ever been told that before. Some said he was handsome. He was strong. He was an ass. Good in bed. A great hugger. Compassionate. He never had a woman tell him he smelled nice. He liked it.

"Thanks." He pulled on his jacket. "I'll set some wood by the door."

"I appreciate that." She slowly closed it behind him.

He walked away smiling and turned his head to smell his collar. It didn't smell like anything to him. Scratch that. It smelled like her. Sweet and fruity and all woman. Something told him his status quo had changed.

CHAPTER FIVE

Samantha stretched her arms over her head. One by one, her verte-brae popped into place. At twenty-nine, she felt more like sixty. Years of pushing her body to the limit were taking their toll.

Last night she was strung too tight to sleep, so she unloaded her car and organized what little she had. Thankfully, Deanna thought about essentials like bedding and towels and toilet paper and hangers. She'd bought soap and shampoo and even put a six-pack of diet soda in the refrigerator. But a can of carbonated liquid wasn't going to stop the growling in her stomach. She needed food, and right away.

After a quick cold shower, she pulled on a pair of yoga pants, a plain pink T-shirt and the hoodie she acquired at last night's concert.

A jog into town would get her blood pumping and warm her up. She knew she had a small window of time to remain unnoticed. Someone was sure to recognize her, and then her peaceful retreat would turn into a paparazzi paradise. She had to take advantage of her anonymity while she had it.

After a quick peek out the door to make sure she hadn't already been discovered, she tucked the strands of her hair into the hoodie and took off at a slow pace.

The altitude and lack of oxygen made her breathe deeply. The cold air burned her lungs. Her tennis shoes crunched the pine needles underfoot. She couldn't remember the last time she'd felt this good. There was no one here to control her choices. Today, she was the ruler of her world.

One foot in front of the other, she listened to the thump of her shoes hitting the hard ground. The air smelled like Christmas, with a hint of pine mixed with campfire.

First stop would be the beauty shop. She had folded a handful of twenties and tucked them inside her pocket in case they had an opening. Would it be the same owner, Kathy, who had fixed her hair years ago? She thought back to that day.

In hopes of saving her mom a few bucks, Samantha decided to cut her own bangs. How hard could it be, she thought? She lifted them up and took the scissors to them. Too bad she had a crooked eye. When she let them loose, one side hovered above her eyebrow and the other skimmed her cheek. She knew she shouldn't have another go of it or she'd be bald when she finished. She walked to the shop and told the owner she'd work for a trim. After cleaning up the hair from the floor, Kathy not only fixed her bangs, but she washed, conditioned and styled it. For Samantha, it was her first spa-like experience.

A strand of blue hair slipped from the hoodie. She tucked it back inside as she neared the town. Yep, getting back to her natural color was a priority. She'd have a better chance of remaining hidden if her hair wasn't so bold.

As she approached the shop, her heart sank. It no longer had the images of scissors and a comb on the window. No lights were on. The glass was whitewashed to hide the vacant interior. Kathy's was no longer in business. *Now what?*

Her stomach gurgled, then growled to remind her that a hamburger and fries from yesterday couldn't hold her forever. She lifted her nose in the air and breathed in the sweet aroma of baked goods. Figuring the smell came from the diner, she moved down the street and found it was also closed.

Hands fisted on her hips, she looked around the town. It wasn't the bustling place she remembered. There were no kids running on the sidewalk. The stores weren't open selling their goods. It was like the town had dried up and disappeared. Her day moved from bad to worse.

Against her better judgment, she looked at her phone this morning. The first ten messages were from her manager, demanding to know where she was. She sent a quick text, informing him she was taking a break. After the next five messages arrived filled with expletives and threats, she powered down her phone and went about her day. What she didn't see couldn't hurt her, or so she told herself. She banished thoughts of work from her brain and went in search of sustenance.

Wanting something sweeter and more satisfying than bad news, she followed the yummy aroma filling the air. Bea, the nice woman who owned the bakery at the end of the block came to mind. On the way down the sidewalk, Samantha reminisced about her short stay in Aspen Cove.

Two days a week, she had walked into town. Mondays she picked up milk from the Corner Store, and Thursdays she bought a loaf of bread. She supposed she could have done it all on the same day, but that would mean one less cookie and one less hug from Bea. She could use a hug about now.

Her heart leaped with joy when she looked across the street at the end of the block to see the bakery open. Would Bea remember her?

Feeling buoyed by fond memories, she skipped across the road and picked up her pace. The closer she got, the sweeter the air smelled. She closed her eyes and breathed deeply. If she was right, it was banana nut muffin day.

One thing Samantha could count on was consistency when it

came to Bea. Every day of the week had a specific muffin. You could schedule your life by the muffin of the day. Today was Sunday.

The bell above the door rang when she entered. A voice from the back called out, "I'll be right with you." It was too young to be Bea, but maybe her daughter. She remembered the girl who worked side-by-side with her mom. A friendly girl with a heart of gold, brown hair, and eyes the color of maple syrup.

One look around told her things had changed everywhere. The pinstriped wallpaper was gone, as were the needlepoint pictures Bea stitched while waiting for her next customer.

The coat of yellow paint made it fresh and bright, but it still felt warm and welcoming. The iron tables with their torn plastic cushions were the same, along with the glass display case and turn of the century cash register. Those little pieces of history made it feel right.

Next to the window sat a woman with her head hung low. She hovered over a sticky note and scribbled while she nibbled on a muffin.

"Hey, sorry about that." A blonde came out of the back wiping her hands on her apron. "I can't figure out how to have the dishes wash themselves."

"That would be awesome." In Samantha's case, it was magical. One minute they were there, the next they were gone. It was like a dish fairy waved a magical wand, but that kind of magic came with a high price.

The blonde stared and gave her a knowing smile. "You're—"

"Starving," she said. Samantha gave her a pleading look and nodded toward the woman at the table. "Banana nut muffin day, right?" Samantha looked at the case that was chock full of treats. There were cookies and brownies and mini loaf cakes. She'd entered the forbidden temple and wasn't leaving until she'd tasted something she wasn't normally allowed.

"Yes. How do you know? You're not—"

"From here?" She picked up a sample from the tray and popped it into her mouth. The banana flavor rushed over her taste buds. She swore she'd tasted heaven. "I lived here for a brief time when I was a kid."

The blonde's eyes lit up. "No way. I can't believe it. Aspen Cove has its own ..." she leaned in and whispered, "superstar."

Samantha gave her an aw-shucks look. "It's not as glamorous as one would think. Besides, there are quite of few memorable people here in Aspen Cove." She thought about Dalton Black and how he looked with muscles rippling and bulging in front of her while he tended the fire. Ink she wanted to explore peeked from under his cotton T-shirt. Dalton started more than the blaze in the fireplace. He'd stirred a spark inside her she thought had died long ago. "Is Bea around?"

The blonde's face fell. "You want a muffin and a coffee?"

Samantha nodded. "Yes, that sounds good." It wasn't often she got to be around strangers and enjoy being anonymous.

"I'm Katie. Katie Bishop. You might remember the Bishop boys, Cannon and Bowie. Bowie is my husband." She put a few muffins on a plate and a pod in the coffeemaker before pressing start.

"I remember them. Big handsome boys."

"Now big, handsome men." Katie smiled. "We have so much to talk about." She pointed to the table opposite the other woman.

A minute later, she came from behind the counter with two cups of coffee and a plate full of goodies.

"You asked about Bea?" There was a minute of silence as she seemed to weigh her words. "I'm afraid she's no longer with us. She passed early last year."

Samantha's heart sank into her empty stomach. As hungry as she was, she wasn't sure she could eat after hearing such sad news.

"That's heartbreaking. She was kind to me."

"Everyone has nice things to say about her."

"Along with her cookies, she always had a smile, a hug, and something positive to say. What about her daughter? I can't remember her name."

Again, Katie frowned. Her hand went to her chest. "Brandy. She's also gone, but she remains in my heart."

"Oh lord. How?"

"Car accident."

"So sad."

"It is, but their memories live on." Katie leaned forward and in a hushed voice said, "Since you're trying to remain incognito, what do you want to be called? I can't very well call you Indigo."

Samantha reached under the hoodie to make sure none of her hair had fallen loose. "I would appreciate it if you didn't. That's not who I am, only who I pretend to be. My real name is Samantha."

"Well, Samantha, since we're going to be friends, eat up and tell me why you're here."

"I needed down time. I'm tired. Burned out, really."

"Where are you staying?"

"I bought a small cabin on Lake Circle next door to Dalton Black. Do you know him?" Samantha imagined everyone knew everybody, but since she didn't know Katie, there was a slim chance Katie didn't know Dalton.

Katie plucked the top off one muffin. "Not only are we friends, we're neighbors. I live on the other side of Dalton." She took a bite and swallowed. "I'm sure glad I covered for Ben today, otherwise, I would have missed you. He normally works Sunday, but he's taken the week off."

"Ben? Cannon and Bowie's dad? I remember him. Nice man. His wife taught at the school."

Another frown. "She's gone, too. Same car accident."

Samantha sipped her coffee and leaned back. "So much has changed."

"Change is the one thing you can always count on."

"Speaking of change." She reached inside the hood and drew a strand of hair free. "I can't lie low with this." She twisted the hair around her finger. "What happened to the beauty shop?"

Katie shrugged. "More change, I guess." In a normal toned voice, she said, "There's a place called Gracie's in Copper Creek. I haven't been there, but I pass it on my way to Target."

The woman across the room rose. Her chair scraped against the linoleum floor. "Don't go to Gracie's." She walked over to Samantha and Katie's table. "You'll pay too much, and she doesn't do good work." With one tug, she yanked down Sam's hoodie and touched her hair. "I can do it for you. You need a touch up, or are you going for something different?"

Katie tilted her head and looked at the woman. "You do hair?"

She nodded. Samantha noticed the dark circles under her eyes and the fading green bruise on her cheekbone. Although Samantha had never been hit, she saw firsthand what it did to a person. Covering her mother's marks was a superpower no eight-year-old girl should have to master.

"Have a seat," Katie offered.

The woman shook her head. "I was leaving my wish. It costs nothing to wish, right? It's like dreaming out loud." She reached over Katie's head and thumbtacked a folded note to the corkboard.

"Your wish?" Samantha asked. She looked above her to the sign on the corkboard that read 'Wishing Wall'. "What's the Wishing Wall?"

Katie laughed. "I started it as a way to get to know the people of Aspen Cove. It was a simple way for people to make reasonable wishes come true. If it's a request for prayer, I pray. If it's something easy, I figure out a way to grant it. All I can do is try. I can't solve all the world's problems, but I can fix a few."

The woman looked at her wish and hung her head. "I fear mine is unobtainable, unreasonable really, but I believe thoughts are important, and I'm trying to find inner peace and a positive outlook." She looked at Samantha and Katie. "I'll leave you two alone."

"Nonsense." Katie rose from her seat and rushed behind the counter for another cup of coffee. "Join us." When she returned, she patted the chair next to her. "Please. Come sit down. What's your name?"

'Skittish' was the only way to describe the dark-haired woman. She looked at them and then at the door as if calculating how many steps it would take her to get there. She took a seat and brought the fresh coffee to her lips.

"I'm Marina."

They introduced themselves and went back to talking hair.

"I want to go back to my natural dark brown."

Marina touched Sam's hair again, moving it between her fingers. "It's healthy despite the heavy processing. I can stop by your place Tuesday if you don't mind me working from your kitchen."

"You don't work in a shop?"

Marina chewed on her inner cheek before she spoke. "Like you, I'm in transition."

Samantha groaned. The more people who recognized her, the less time she'd have. "You women from Aspen Cove are too observant. I'm begging you to please not give me away."

Katie covered both Samantha's and Marina's hands with hers. "Aspen Cove takes care of its own."

Marina shook her head. "I'm not from here."

"You're an honorary resident. Besides, maybe someday you'll move here. There's an empty beauty shop across the street." Katie touched her blonde hair. "We're all in need of your services."

For the first time since Samantha entered the bakery, she saw Marina smile. She had a strong urge to hug her but didn't want to send her running.

"Tuesday sounds great." She took a wad of twenties from her pocket and laid them on the table. "Here's money to get what you need. I live at 7 Lake Circle. What time are we doing this?"

Marina glanced at the pile of cash on the table. "I can be there at eleven. You want a dark rich brown, right?"

Samantha flicked the hoodie back over her head. "I'll settle for anything other than blue."

After she finished her muffin and coffee, she paid her bill and made her way home. When she arrived at the cabin, she was greeted with a pleasant surprise. Maybe her day was turning around.

Pantry staples like bread, eggs, milk, and sugar sat tucked inside a cooler on her porch. Next to it was a vase of flowers and a note.

Welcome to the neighborhood, Samantha. Thought you could use a few items for your empty cupboards. The flowers looked like a nice add, too. Wanted to say I'm sorry one more time for bulldozing you.

Dalton

She brought the mixed bouquet to her nose and inhaled. For a second, they didn't smell like flowers at all. She imagined they smelled like him. Raw energy mixed with hot male and evergreen.

A lot had changed in Aspen Cove, but one thing remained the same. Just like when she was a kid, Samantha would be happy to spend hours looking at Dalton Black.

CHAPTER SIX

"You realize I'm not really a killer, right?" Dalton leaned forward and placed his arms on the parole officer's desk. She was a nice woman who insisted he call her Lucy. In his head, she'd always be Ms. Warwick. He'd never had a parole officer before her and didn't know if they were all as kind and flexible, but he appreciated her meeting him on a Sunday afternoon.

"I'm not here to judge you. I'm here to make sure you toe the line. You behaving yourself, Dalton?"

"Yes, ma'am. Can't get into too much trouble in Aspen Cove."

She leaned back and kicked her boots up onto the table. "It's been my experience that if you're looking for trouble, you can find it anywhere."

He shook his head. "I'm not looking for anything but an end to this nightmare."

She pushed off the desk, sending her chair rolling back. Leaning forward, she opened his file. "It's been a year without problems. I don't imagine I'll be seeing you as much next year."

She pulled a black pen from the edge of her desk and marked up the page. "Have you done anything about that anger problem?"

"I had six years of incarceration. Do you think that helps anger issues?"

"You telling me you're still angry?"

He shook his head. He was pissed, but it wasn't something he'd share with her. "What I'm telling you is, I didn't have anger problems going in, and I didn't have them coming out."

She laughed. "Good line. I'll write that one down." She shuffled through his papers. "I know what went down that night. I've read all the transcripts. Some would call you a hero—others a vigilante. Me, I'd call you a nice guy who thought he was doing the right thing."

He couldn't argue, she was right. People either loved him or hated him. There was no gray area to killing a person. "Imagine that. Chivalry is dead."

"It isn't dead. Just misunderstood. Don't stop caring for people. That's when the trouble *really* begins."

Trouble for him started when he cared. He'd played out all the roles he could have taken that night in his head again and again. He could have been the pretender who ignored the woman's cries when that asshole punched her. He could have been the ignorant ass who stood to the side and watched it all go down while laughing and saying she probably deserved it. He could have been a lot of things, but he was the only man who stepped forward to stop another man from beating a woman because she ignored his advances.

Dalton caught Andy Kranz's fist midair as he tried to deliver the second blow to Bethany Waters. When Andy turned around, it wasn't to apologize. He swung with his other fist and landed a solid blow to Dalton's gut. Dalton fisted up and took one swing at the drunk bastard. He hit him right between the eyes. The jerk dropped like a boulder. The problem was, he never got back up.

"Bethany Waters wrote at least a hundred letters to the courts and parole board." Lucy pulled out a stack of photocopied letters.

Dalton and Lucy had never talked about the crime, only the sentence. It was interesting to hear her take on things.

"I know. She sent me about two hundred in prison." He had them rubber banded together. It helped him to know he'd done the right thing even though the outcome wasn't what he expected. "She still writes occasionally to say thanks. She's married and has two kids."

"What about you? You seeing anyone?"

Lucy was pushing sixty. Life hadn't been kind to her. Her leathered skin was marked by the lines of a life lived outdoors. Her calloused hands were rough enough to sand wood. During one of their talks, she'd told him she raised champion horses. Serving as a parole officer was her way of giving back.

"You flirting with me, Lucy?"

"Darlin', I'd rip you to pieces. You couldn't handle me. Go find yourself a nice young thing and make babies."

This time, he laughed. "My dating resume is tarnished. Few women are looking for ex-felons who cook blue plate specials part-time at a diner."

"You don't come out of the gate with 'Hi, I'm Dalton Black, and I did six years for killing someone.'" She pursed her lips, which made her entire face prune up. "That's like telling a guy you have herpes before you even kiss him."

His mouth fell open. The one thing Dalton liked most about Lucy was her candor. She didn't pussyfoot around or tell him life would be wonderful. She usually told him to get his shit together, and she'd see him next month.

"You got herpes?"

"No, I'm giving you an example of what *not* to do. Here's a good one. Don't annoy your PO, or she'll revoke your parole."

"Got it. Are we done?"

She turned to the first page of the folder. "Sober—check. Employed—check. Housed—check. Cute as a button—check." She closed the file. "You can let your past define you, or you can define your future. Who will you become, Dalton Black?"

"Good question, Lucy. I'll give it some thought."

"Don't waste too much time. You're thirty-four. That clock only moves forward."

"Got it." He rose from his chair. "Same day next month?"

"Nope, I'll see you in six." She walked him to the door. "Enjoy your life. Not enough that I'll be barking up your ass, but enough so the years don't pass by with regret."

Dalton climbed into his truck with a lot to think about. Actually, it was a little—a little blue-haired woman who'd been on his mind since he busted through her front door and accused her of a crime.

That bothered him. He'd been quick to judge and condemn. He knew better. He'd been found guilty before he had cuffs on. Visits with Lucy always brought that day into focus. Did he feel bad that Andy Kranz died? Sure. He hadn't intended to kill him, but it came down to Bethany or Andy. In Dalton's mind, the woman would almost always win. Especially when the man was being an asshole.

Having lived in a violent house, the odds were in favor of Dalton being an abuser, but he wasn't. He'd taken a punch or two or twenty from his old man by stepping into the fist before it hit his mother. He had the scars to prove it. The one above his eyebrow was a constant reminder. A reminder of who he never wanted to be.

The three-hour drive from Denver back to Aspen Cove gave him plenty of time to think about the trajectory of his life, but he couldn't clear his head. His mind kept going back to Samantha. He wasn't sure if it was the memory of her staring at him from the front of the bus in their youth or the exhaustion he saw when she collapsed onto her couch. All he wanted to do was feed her and make her happy because for one second last night when she smiled, his entire world seemed brighter.

When he pulled into his driveway and hopped out of his truck, he glanced to the right. The house looked empty and lifeless in the twilight of the night. That was until he heard a soft lilting voice and the strum of a guitar coming from the beach.

Instead of going inside like he planned, he walked quietly around the back to find Samantha sitting on the ground, facing the lake. The sun had set, and the bruised sky hung above her head with wisps of pink and purple and blue.

Too far away to hear the lyrics, he leaned against his deck and listened to the blend of chords mixed with her angelic voice. There was a beautiful woman, good music, a picturesque setting. The only thing missing was a glass of wine. That was one thing he could provide.

He returned to the beach in minutes with an opened bottle of cabernet and two glasses. The damp dirt ate up any noise his shoes made. Behind her, he cleared his throat. She jumped six inches into the air.

She swung around, brandishing her guitar like a weapon. When she saw it was him, she lowered it and tugged it to her chest. "Holy hell, you scared me near to death. I could have hurt you."

Dalton had never seen a person move so fast. "Are you going to bludgeon me to death with your guitar?"

She lowered herself back to the folded blanket. "Murder doesn't look good on a resume."

Never a truer statement had been said. He lifted the wine and the glasses. "I saw you and thought a good wine would go great with the sunset."

"Dalton Black, be careful, or I might think you're wooing me."

"Well, that's something I've never been accused of." He walked over and took a seat on the damp ground beside her. "Care for a glass?"

She set her guitar down and slid over to make room for him. "Get off the wet ground. If you're sharing your wine, I can share my blanket."

He was twice her size and took up most of the space. The urge to pick her up and sit her on his lap was strong, but he controlled his desire. Under the half-hung moon, he filled the glasses and offered a toast. "Here's to celebrating."

"What are we celebrating?" She turned to him. Her eyes were almost black, with a hint of blue around the edges.

"Milestones," he said, and touched his glass to hers, letting the clink ring in the air.

"Do tell ..." She smiled, and that warmth and light he experienced the night before radiated through him and settled like a fire in his chest.

"Mine are complicated to explain." He heard Lucy's warning about coming out the gate with an *I'm-a-felon* introduction. "What about you? What do you want to celebrate?"

"I have some difficult-to-explain milestones as well. Let's simply agree to celebrate."

"Sounds like a plan."

They sipped their wine and looked at the still water.

"I don't remember the weather being so temperamental. Last night I nearly froze to death, and tonight I barely need a jacket."

"It's early spring. It might have been close to sixty degrees today, but next week we'll get a foot of snow."

"Really?" She leaned forward and rested her chin on her knees. "I lived here from August to early November. At the first big snow storm, we headed out." She shivered and pulled down her sleeves.

He wasn't sure if she was cold or living a dark memory. He moved closer until their bodies touched on one side from shoulder to ankle.

"It's been a light year for snow. People talk about climate change. And when we go from this to a foot of snow, I get it."

"Other than the possibility of freezing to death, I'd love to see that much snow." She looked to the cloudless night. "To sit in front of a blazing fire with hot cocoa and a good book. That sounds like heaven."

He picked up the bottle and topped off her glass. "You have simple wishes."

She sighed. "I live an incredibly busy life. I'm afraid it will be over before I really get to enjoy it."

"I get the impression you're a workaholic."

She laughed. It was a sweet sound that sent a ripple from his chest to the space between his legs. He was grateful the moon wasn't full. Otherwise, his attraction to her couldn't be hidden.

"Not by choice."

"It's all a choice." Dalton knew that life was a series of decisions. Some set you up for success. Others could ruin you. "You can choose differently."

"Hence the milestones. Coming here was a risky decision." She leaned into him and traced the tattoos on his arm. "Bet these took thought."

He let out a low, rumbling laugh. "Not at all. Most of them took a night of too much alcohol."

"Seriously?"

"Not all the decisions I've made were wise." He took a chance and wrapped his arm around her shoulder. "Not sure if this decision is wise either, but I really want to kiss you."

"You want to kiss me?" She turned her body and faced him. Her crisscrossed legs caged him from hip to knee.

"More than anything." It had been a long time since he'd kissed anyone out of desire rather than need. That first week of man-whoring after prison didn't count. He'd had six years of celibacy to make up for. All the faces blended together. No one was looking for anything but a good time. Tonight was different. Wanting to kiss her meant something to him.

She lifted her chin in what looked like defiance, but her eyes softened into submission. "I'd like that." She closed them and leaned in.

He pressed his mouth to hers. His tongue slipped out to taste the sweetness of her lips. The angle was awkward. He was too tall. She was too small. This wasn't working. After he lowered his glass to the ground, he took hers and set it aside before he lifted her onto his lap. The exact place he wanted her earlier.

She straddled him and wrapped her legs around his waist. Stone hard thighs pressed into his hips. His hands moved down her too-thin body and gripped an ass made of steel.

"I've never kissed a girl with blue hair."

She whispered against his lips. "Me either."

He chuckled. "That's a relief."

"Are you going to kiss me or talk about my hair?"

"Oh, I'm going to kiss you like you've never been kissed before." He lifted his hands to cup her face and lowered his lips to hers. He knew this was a bad idea, but he'd be damned if he could stop himself from indulging. He nipped at her bottom lip and pulled it into his mouth. He tasted wine and desire ... and maybe a little fear.

Her tiny hands moved up his chest, over his shoulders, and ran through his hair. He reminded himself that women were trouble and the only reason he kissed her was because she said she was leaving. She wouldn't be around long enough to cause him harm.

Samantha opened her mouth and moaned. It was deep and throaty and sexy as hell. That was all the invitation he needed to intensify the kiss. One hand slid up to the back of her head where he threaded his fingers through her hair. He pulled her closer. His tongue stroked hers softly at first and became more demanding as the kiss lingered. He continued his assault on her mouth until he could no longer breathe. The desire he felt for her had sucked all the oxygen from his lungs.

Despite the temperature dropping outside, he was hot. *She* was hot. He pulled away with regret. All he wanted was to get lost in her touch and her taste, but he knew better. He expected a simple kiss, but this was way more than he bargained for. "I should get you inside."

She leaned back and looked at him. What did he see in her eyes? Under the night sky they were like a wishing well, full of dark desire and endless possibilities. Dalton hadn't felt this turned on since he was a teen.

Her legs lowered to the ground, and she rose to her feet. "You're probably right. Thanks for the wine." She looked to her deck. "Oh, and the flowers and eggs and bread and stuff. That was sweet."

"I was being neighborly."

She picked up her guitar. "I think I might like this neighborhood."

He walked her to her door. "I'd like to kiss you again."

47

"Now?" She turned the knob and let the door swing open behind her.

"Hell yes, but I won't because I wouldn't stop at the kiss. Racing to the finish line would be a shame when there's so much to explore in-between." He looked past her to the fireplace. "You want a fire?"

She shook her head. "No, thanks. I'm already warm."

He reached past her and waved his hand through the air. Her cabin was colder inside than it was outdoors. "You're warm now, but it won't last. You have gas heating. You know that, right?"

"I turned it on. It doesn't work."

He pressed into her until she backed into the living room. "My cabin is the same model as yours, only we have flipped floor plans." He walked past her to a hallway closet. "Bring me the matches. The pilot light to your heater probably isn't lit. Didn't you use the stove?"

"No, I went to the bakery." She handed him the box of matches and stood back as he turned on the gas and lit the pilot light. On the hallway wall, he adjusted the thermostat to sixty-eight.

"That should do it. You'll *stay* warm now." He closed the door and looked down at her grateful expression.

"Or you could kiss me again. That seems to heat me up."

"You're trouble." He shook his head and walked out the door.

As he walked toward his place, he mentally kicked himself for walking away from a sure thing. Carelessness sat on one shoulder, screaming, "Turn around!" Common sense sat on the other, demanding he walk away.

He wanted to turn around and run back to her cabin. The problem was, he knew that the minute he did, a kiss would lead to more. And something told him that when he pressed himself inside her body, Samantha White would own his heart.

CHAPTER SEVEN

Even an hour-long run couldn't clear her mind of last night's kiss. The way Dalton's body melded to hers. How his hands sent sparks of awareness racing across her skin. His touch was the final thing she thought of last night and the first thing she had on her mind this morning.

He wanted to explore what happened between the beginning and the end. *Had she ever had that?* The last beginning she had was with the lead singer of Granite Soldiers.

The short fling started last summer when the band opened for her in Europe. Thankfully, it never went further than a few kisses. She'd shown up at his bus unannounced, only to find him the meat between two blonde honey buns.

She ran down Main Street toward the bakery, but the smell of coffee and bacon stopped her in front of the diner. It was Tuesday, which meant breakfast was served. She calculated the distance she had run and imagined she'd burned off enough calories for an egg or a bowl of oatmeal. Old habits were hard to break. *Screw healthy eating.* Today she'd have bacon and whatever else she wanted.

Swiping the sweat from her forehead, she ran her hand around the knit cap that imprisoned her hair. There were no escapees.

Through the swinging doors, she entered a different world. The diner was probably around when she lived here, but she and her mom didn't eat out much. Restaurants were not in their budget. It was funny to think how far she'd come.

A woman approached. She'd recognize Dalton's mom anywhere with her bouffant hairstyle and fire engine red lips. She realized Maisey Black in fact owned Maisey's Diner. Why she hadn't already put that together, she had no idea.

"Have a seat anywhere."

"Thanks, Ms. Black." Samantha looked around the near-empty eatery. The only occupied table was one in the corner. Tucked against the wall, an older man read his paper. The only thing visible was his white hair peeking out in tufts above the pages.

Samantha took the corner booth on the other side of the restaurant.

Maisey followed her, carrying an empty mug and a full pot of coffee. "It's Bishop now... Do I know you?"

"Congratulations." Besides Cannon and Bowie, there was only one Bishop remaining. She must have married Ben. "I doubt you know me, but I remember you. I lived here briefly with my mom, Yvette."

She put the pot and cup on the table and slid into the bench across from Samantha. "I remember your mom. She worked at the paper mill."

Samantha nodded. "Yes, but then it closed, and the first snow fell and we left."

"And now you're back." She pushed the mug forward. "Coffee?"

"I'd love some." Samantha lived on black coffee and adrenaline.

"How's your mom?"

It had been a while since she'd seen her. Between the travel and recording, she didn't get much time to relax or visit.

"She's great. She lives in San Diego now." The first thing

Samantha purchased once she'd made it was a house for her mom. She never wanted her to have to live in a car or a rent by the week motel room again.

"She married?"

She laughed. "Oh no, she said once was enough for her. My father wasn't a particularly nice man." Samantha recognized the knowing look that spread over Maisey's face.

"I understand." She lifted her hand to her cheek like she had remembered a painful moment. "I hope she's happy."

With a nice little nest egg and a fully paid for house, Samantha hoped she was happy too. "Seems to be."

"You might know my son, Dalton."

Oh boy, do I know him. "Yes, he's my neighbor."

"Is that right? He didn't tell me." She rose from the booth and picked up the pot of coffee. "I'll tell him you're here."

"Wait. He's here?"

"Of course. He's the chef."

Of course he was. It made sense. He told her he was a chef. Only he didn't say where.

Samantha was thrilled with the coffee. Add in a side order of Dalton, and it was a perfect day. The only thing that could make it better would be some of that in-between stuff he spoke about.

She fidgeted in the booth while she waited. Without a stitch of makeup on, she wasn't pretty to look at, but Dalton didn't seem to notice last night. Then again, it was dark. She pinched her cheeks to pink and chanced a side sniff to make sure her deodorant was working. All seemed to be in order when Mr. Tall, Dark, and Delicious walked over.

"Good morning," he said. Those two words that could have been a lover's sonnet to a woman who had so much, and yet so little.

"Hey, you." She knew she looked at him like he was breakfast. "I didn't know you worked here."

"The exchange of resumes didn't seem necessary."

She blushed under his gaze. "I suppose we shared enough."

He laughed loud enough for the old man in the corner to lower his newspaper and frown.

Dalton hovered over her. "You think that was enough? Baby, that wasn't even an appetizer." His breath floated over her. Goosebumps rose on her skin, but the heat of desire pulsed through her veins.

She took him in from head to toe. His hair was covered with a dark bandana. The black cotton of his T-shirt stretched across his broad chest, reminding her of every muscle her fingertips skimmed over last night. Worn jeans hung low on his hips and led to black boots more suited for a motorcycle ride than a kitchen.

Her hands tingled to touch him. Afraid she'd act on her desires, she tucked them beneath her legs.

"Why are you hiding in the corner?"

"I'm not hiding." In fact, she was. With her back to the window and her body pressed against the red vinyl, she hoped to disappear into the décor. One reason she chose Aspen Cove was because it was the last place anyone would look for her. Few people knew of her connection to the small town. "I smelled bacon and came in to investigate."

"You hungry?" He licked his lips like he could taste her on the air.

"Are you going to stand over me and tease me or satisfy my hunger?"

His big body pushed into the booth, trapping her between him and the wall. His arm fell over her shoulder while his lips traced her jaw to the shell of her ear. "What are you hungry for?"

Laughter bubbled until it burst forth. "Does that work for you?" It worked for her, but she wasn't ready to strip down and be devoured in a diner. Someone had to put an end to the madness before she asked him to kick everyone out and hang out the 'closed' sign.

He sat back and watched her with his soulful blue eyes. "I'm a little rusty in the seduction department."

She twisted so her knee pressed into his thigh. "Are you now?" She lifted her hand and brushed it across his perfectly trimmed beard. "You're selling yourself short. I loved the flowers. The eggs and milk were a unique treat but much appreciated. The wine and the kiss on the beach? That was foreplay."

He twisted his lips in a thoughtful expression. "Flowers, food, and wine, huh?" He scooted out of the booth and stood. "I've got you covered." He whipped around and walked into the kitchen.

Something told Samantha she'd unleashed a monster. As she drank her coffee, she powered up her phone and read through the next twenty-two emails that started with "Where the hell are you?" and ended with her agent pleading for her to contact Dave.

She knew she started a panic when she left. They wanted a new contract. A five-year deal that would give them control over her life again. It wasn't happening. She'd given them enough.

She dialed Deanna and waited for her to pick up.

"Are you okay?" were the first words out of her mouth.

"I'm perfect. Still incognito. Getting hair color today."

"Ooh, what color?"

"Boring brown."

"Nothing about you is boring."

"Oh please. Boring is my middle name, but I'm working on that." She touched her lips and sighed. "I met a guy my first night here." She refused to say he accosted her because what came next was far more exciting. "We shared a bottle of wine and an amazing kiss."

"Does he know who you are?"

"No, and that was what made the kiss that much more amazing."

"Don't get your heart broken. You're not staying there. Aspen Cove was supposed to be like rehab for your soul. You can't keep him."

Deanna was right. Aspen Cove wasn't part of her long-term plan. The plan was to rest so she could get back into the recording studio to sing what she wanted to sing. She needed to find a studio willing to piss off Oliver Shepherd. Ending her relationship with the music mogul could blacklist her for life. It might come down to her starting her own label.

"I know, and it's been good so far."

"Tell me about that kiss."

"The kiss," she closed her eyes to remember it better, "was amazing."

A plate of food appeared in front of her. "'Amazing,' huh?" His warm molasses voice seeped into her cells, heating her all the way to her core.

"Got to go, Deanna. The kisser is here." She hung up before her assistant could say another word.

Dalton sat across from her and plucked a piece of bacon from her plate. She looked down at what he brought to the table. It was more like a platter than a plate.

"You better have more than a piece of bacon. Who do you think will eat all of this?"

"You are. You're way too thin. While your ass is perfection, the rest of you is like a piece of knotty pine."

Samantha's chin nearly hit her chest. "That can't work for you."

He rose from his seat and moved next to her. "It's not my intention to offend you, but you have to know you're painfully thin."

Barely over a hundred pounds, she was thin. "I have a killer metabolism."

"Then eat up. You'll need it."

"For?"

"There's a bonfire and barbecue tonight on the beach. We're celebrating Sage and Cannon's engagement. I thought maybe you could go with me?"

She looked up into his eyes. Eyes that threatened to melt her. "Dalton Black, are you asking my knotty-pine ass on a date?"

He thumbed her chin so she couldn't look away. "No. I'm inviting the woman who has an ass created in heaven and hip bones as sharp as anvils on a date."

"So, I'm *not* knotty?"

He pulled his lower lip into his mouth and rolled it between his teeth. When it popped free, he leaned forward and brushed his mouth over hers. "God, I hope you're naughty."

The bell above the door rang, and a large family entered.

"That's my cue to leave. See you tonight?" His expression was full of hope.

"I'll be there."

She'd say whatever he wanted to hear in order to see that smile again.

Samantha glanced at the family and thought the mom and dad looked familiar, but she couldn't come up with a name. The double doors to the kitchen swung closed when Dalton walked through them and opened again when Maisey walked out and greeted the couple and their seven children. That was a couple who spent a lot of time enjoying the "in-between."

Maisey hugged the woman and patted the telltale bump on her stomach. Baby number eight was on its way.

As a performer, she never had the time to consider marriage or children, but looking at the family in front of her caused a pang of jealousy to thread through her. She never asked for fame and fortune. She asked for a life. Maybe she should have been more specific.

CHAPTER EIGHT

An hour later, Samantha sat at her kitchen table while Marina inspected her hair. She talked about a two-step process that included bleaching and dying or something of that nature. All Samantha cared about was blending in.

"I appreciate you making a house call."

Marina gave her a weak smile. "I could use the distraction." She lifted her arms, making her shirt rise up. The bruises on her stomach had faded to a pale yellow.

"There are places you can go for help."

At first, Samantha thought Marina would ignore her comment, but in fact, she considered her answer. "This is not what you think."

"My imagination is pretty active and often accurate. My father abused my mother. We escaped but looked over our shoulders for years. How sad is it that the day he died was the day our lives began?"

Marina unpacked a bag of supplies and covered Samantha's shoulders with a navy blue cape. Why did women insist on protecting their abusers? It was obvious Marina had suffered some kind of trauma. "Are you running from something? Someone?"

"Are you?" she countered. "There are many kinds of abuse. They all hurt the same."

Samantha considered her words. Bruises healed, but the words stayed inside and beat you up repeatedly. Abuse was abuse no matter what form it came in.

Cool liquid gushed from a bottle onto her hair. "Why do you stay?"

"Why did you?"

She hated it when people answered questions with questions. "It took time to get a plan together."

"Ditto." That was the end of the conversation. Marina worked in silence as Samantha thought about her own life. Coming to Aspen Cove was the beginning, but not the end.

Two hours later, she looked at herself in the mirror. Samantha White was back.

Marina had breathed new life into her tired persona. She couldn't wait to show off her true self. Would Dalton like her hair now that it was brown, or was it the edginess of the blue that attracted him?

"You have no idea what you did for me today." Samantha handed her several hundred dollars.

"That's too much." She tried to pass back everything but a hundred.

Samantha closed her hand over the hand of the woman who had given her a fresh start. "Put it to work in your plan."

Marina looked down at the pile of twenties. When her head lifted, tears filled her eyes. "You have no idea what this means."

Samantha pulled her in for a hug. "You'd be surprised."

As soon as the hairdresser left, Samantha found herself back in front of the mirror, staring at her reflection. How had things gotten so out of hand that she'd let another person define who she was?

Her thoughts went to Marina. Desperation made people do crazy things. Samantha didn't know why smart women stayed in bad situations. Society would say they were dumb, but when the options came down to living or dying, the choice got easier. When your choice is between dying by starvation or dying at the hand of an asshole, the choice was less clear because the outcome remained the same.

In many ways, Samantha had already experienced death. The beatings her mom took were the death of her childhood. Signing a long-term contract was the death of her choices. Now Samantha White was back and ready to live again.

She applied blush, mascara, and lip gloss before getting dressed for the bonfire. An internal debate warred inside her on whether she should wear nice jeans or worn jeans. It was funny how worn jeans cost twice as much for less fabric. A good shredding cost big bucks these days. She paired the torn jeans with a white T-shirt and hoodie. The weather had stayed in the mid-sixties all day and only now dipped down to the fifties. With a fire pit and a hot man, Samantha was certain she'd stay plenty warm.

Dalton said it was a date, but did he mean a *date-date* or a *come-hang-out-with-me date*?

Deanna's words echoed in her head. *"You can't keep him."* Maybe not, but she could enjoy him for a while, couldn't she? At least she could enjoy his kisses. That was probably the smartest plan. Don't let it get past a hug or a kiss or two ... or ten. He was an excellent kisser, and Samantha found no reason to waste those talents.

She heard voices and music coming from the lake side of her property. Her stomach grumbled, and she hoped they would serve food. All she'd eaten was the breakfast Dalton had cooked. It was enough to feed an army, but not enough to last her all day.

She grabbed a piece of bread and walked outside. Several people milled about the property two doors down. She leaned against the deck rail and watched as Katie talked and laughed with a tiny redhead.

A tall man came up behind Katie and kissed her on the cheek. She'd recognize him anywhere. Bowie Bishop always commanded attention. When he stepped around his wife, he handed her a baby.

Katie never mentioned a child, but then again they had shared little beyond baked goods and hair stories. The way she cooed over the infant twisted Samantha's stomach into knots. It was obvious the child was adored, and the parents were in love. Had her mother ever had a single moment of such bliss? Would she?

Out of the corner of her eye, she saw movement. A big lumbering bear of a man hopped off his deck and headed her way. She could smell his cologne before he arrived. It was a mix of clean linen and citrus.

"You ready?" He took the steps up to her deck two at a time. In front of her, he stood still and stared. "Wow." He ran his fingers through the hair that floated over her shoulder. "Done with that phase of your life?"

Phase was right. "Yep, this is the real me. Still want that date?"

He pulled his lower lip between his teeth. It was the sexiest thing she'd seen in a long time. There would definitely be more kisses.

"You're beautiful."

She'd been told that a lot, but not by anyone that mattered, and somehow, Dalton mattered. Was it because she'd had a twelve-week crush on him as a kid? Or was it because he still didn't know who she was and he liked her anyway?

"I am?" she asked sweetly. "I wasn't sure you'd like it."

He pulled her back from the rail and pressed her against the wall in the dark corner of her deck. "This is how much I like it." Hidden in the shadows, he kissed her senseless. How his kisses could suck the air from her lungs and weaken her knees was a mystery. No kiss she could remember had ever been so powerful. It was like she found her next breath in his lungs. She never wanted to break the kiss.

He stood back and licked his lips. "Grape?"

She nodded. Cheap lip gloss was her guilty pleasure. Deanna bought it in bulk from Walmart. "I have watermelon, too."

She felt like a teenager, not a twenty-nine-year-old woman.

"I'd love to taste that as well."

"It can be arranged." He looked over his shoulder at the group growing around the bonfire. "Are you ready to meet the gang?"

Am I? Indigo screamed, "No," but Samantha stood tall and said, "Yes. I can't wait to meet everyone." A knot of fear tugged at her insides. Had Katie told anyone who she was? That was the problem with fame. It was hard to tell who were true friends. Hard to know who was trustworthy. Hard to get close to people.

Dalton ran his tongue across her lower lip. "I think I got it all. I'm ready to test the watermelon."

She pushed at his chest. "You ate all my gloss." She pulled the tube from her back pocket and applied a new coat.

"I knew you'd have me covered." He dipped down for another quick kiss before he folded his hand around hers and led her to his friends.

Katie was the first to rush over. She adjusted her hold on her baby and gave Samantha a side hug. "You came. Dalton said he invited you."

Dalton let his fingers run languidly across her lower back. The touch sent a kinetic energy zipping through her. She felt truly alive. "I'll be right back," he said and disappeared into the house behind them, leaving her missing him already.

"I hope it's okay that I'm crashing your party."

"You're making it better." Katie's eyes went to Samantha's hair. "Marina has some skills." She walked around Samantha, checking out the color from all angles. "It looks so natural."

"She did a good job. It's exactly how I remember my hair used to be." Samantha couldn't stop twirling a lock around her finger. It felt so soft and thick and ... like *her.*

"Did she say much to you while she was at your house?" Katie looked down at her bundled up baby and smiled.

"No, she was friendly but reserved."

Katie's smile turned upside down. "I looked at her wish."

"It's none of my business, but is it grantable?"

She shook her head. "Not really. It was cryptic. All it said was she needed a plan B. Did you get the impression that she was in trouble?"

"The bruises on her face were my first clue, but she has to help herself before anyone else can help her." Samantha knew that from experience.

She looked down at the baby sleeping in Katie's arms.

"You want to hold her?"

As strange as it might be, Samantha had never held a baby in her life. They appeared so tiny and frail and complicated. "No, that's okay."

Katie had already shifted the baby forward, leaving her no choice but to offer up the cradle of her arms. "She won't break. Her name is Sahara. She's my little miracle."

Samantha held the baby with stiff arms. Although differently shaped, she wasn't much heavier than Deanna's poodle—but Sahara was so much cuter. "How old is she?"

"About three months."

"She's beautiful." Samantha lifted the bundled baby and smelled the scent everyone talked about. Babies had a smell all their own that was pure heaven. "You say she's a miracle?"

"Long story, but I'll give you the short version." Katie told her tale about two women, one heart, the perfect man, passionate love, and faith.

"Holy shit. I can't even write stuff that good."

"You did." She looked around as if to make sure no one was in earshot. "Your song 'Empty Box' is one of my favorites."

Dalton approached carrying a glass of wine and a beer. "Which one would you like?"

Samantha gave Katie the baby back and took the wine from Dalton. "I'll stick with what I know. Besides, wine has fewer calories."

Dalton quirked a brow and switched drinks with her, handing

her the beer. "You need the calories. Did you eat anything else today?"

Katie looked at them with curiosity and smiled. "Got a protector already. Dalton's a keeper."

With little thought, Samantha blurted, "Oh, I can't keep him. I won't be here that long."

If frowns could darken the moment, Samantha stood in pitch black. Katie shrugged and nodded toward the redhead walking toward them. "That's what Sage said, and it's been a year."

"I hear we have a new resident." Sage walked over to Samantha and offered her a handshake.

"Yes, I'm Samantha White."

Sage laughed a full belly laugh. "We've got a White," she looked at Dalton, "and a Black." She stood next to Katie and wrapped her arm around her shoulder. It was obvious they were friends. Samantha hoped that someday she could stay somewhere long enough to make lasting connections. "Looks like we have to be the gray in-between."

Katie shook her head. "No way, gray isn't my color."

Samantha watched Sage for any hint of recognition. There wasn't any. If she knew who Samantha was, she was good at hiding the knowledge.

"Doc is on the deck, grilling burgers," Sage said.

Katie looked over her shoulder. "Last time he was the grill master, I found out I was pregnant. Who's next?" She looked at Sage and Samantha who had stepped back several feet.

"I know what causes that," Sage said. "I'm protected from that particular problem." They all turned toward Samantha.

"Don't look at me. There are certain activities that one has to take part in to ... you know. I haven't taken part in quite some time." The heat of a blush raced across her cheeks. She'd just told several strangers she'd been celibate.

Katie and Sage looked surprised. Dalton looked pleased. "Let's feed you." He rested his hand on the small of her back and walked her up the steps to where an old guy manned the grill. The man from the diner.

"Doc, this is our newest resident, Samantha White."

Doc looked her up and down and shook his head. He plated her up a hot dog and a burger, then reached inside a bag of chips and dumped a super-sized serving on her plate. "Eat up, young lady. You're too thin."

Samantha gasped and looked at Dalton. "Have you been talking to him?"

Doc laughed. "You think she's thin too?" Doc gave her another look. "I'd guess a hundred pounds fully clothed."

Feeling the need to defend her physique, she said, "One hundred and four, bare-assed naked."

Doc forked another dog and slapped it on her plate. "Eat up, young lady. From the look on Dalton's face, you're going to need it."

"Oh my God." She marched away with two hot dogs, a hamburger, and a mountain of chips. She took a seat on the ground a few feet away from the frozen lake.

Before she knew it, two dogs bounded forward. She held her plate of food in the air while the canines tried to lick her to death.

"Otis. Bishop. Down, boys." Dalton shooed the dogs away. The chocolate lab chased after the three-legged retriever.

"I wanted to be the one to kiss you before dinner." Dalton sank to the ground beside her.

She tried to mimic the stern tone of his voice. "Dalton. Down, boy."

He looked at her plate, piled a mile high. "How about we share that?"

"What? Are you afraid my knotty-pine ass will get too big if I eat it all?"

"Your ass is perfect. Let's forget I said you were skinny. I'd like to take it back." He took the plate of food and set it next to her. He pushed the beer bottle into the soft ground beside her where he also put the glass of wine. "Let's start over."

"Okay." She smiled. "Hi, I'm Samantha White, and I heard you are a perfect kisser."

He held her hands. "Hello, Samantha White, I'm Dalton Black, and I think you're perfect all around." He leaned in and brushed his lips over hers. "I know you're not staying, but maybe while you're here we can be friends." He gave her a heart-stopping smile.

"Does that friendship include kisses?"

"We can negotiate as we go."

They sat together in front of the lake, which quickly became her favorite place. They ate and laughed and talked. All the Bishop couples joined them. There was Sage and Cannon, Ben and Maisey, and Katie and Bowie. Then Doc joined, followed by Otis, who was happy to gobble up leftovers until Bishop took over.

She'd escaped to Aspen Cove to rest, or so she thought, but maybe she'd come here to think. Being surrounded by people who cared about each other was plenty to provoke her musings.

At the end of the evening, Dalton walked her back to her place. He hadn't kissed her once since that brief touch earlier. He'd been the perfect gentleman. She wondered if her intent to leave was the reason he kept his distance.

"How are those supplies holding up?"

"You want to talk about food?"

"No, I wanted to tell you I'm heading to Copper Creek to pick up a few things tomorrow. Do you want to come with me?"

Everything about Dalton screamed "sexy"—from the way he licked a drop of wine from his lips to the way he watched her eat her hot dog. He said, "Come with me" like it was an offer of more than a ride into town.

"Mr. Black, are you asking me out on a second date?" His boyish smile belied the hulking man in front of her.

"I think I might be. That leaves us one away from our third. You know what they say about third dates ..."

She knew exactly what they said. Third dates were the put-out-or-get-out date. "Are you really a third-date-rule man?"

"There are rules?" He kissed her cheek. "I was going to say on the third date, I'd show you my skills." He waited a moment, knowing full well what that implied. "My culinary skills, that is. I'll cook for you." He turned and walked away.

He was long gone, but she stared at where he had stood. Dalton Black knew she was leaving and planned to woo her anyway.

CHAPTER NINE

Normally, he didn't pay much attention to what he wore. Today, he stood in his closet and looked at the rainbow of T-shirts in front of him. He was spending the day with Samantha. He didn't know why that made him so happy, but it did.

She said she was leaving, which he understood. Aspen Cove didn't have much to offer, but he hoped she'd change her mind.

He tugged the bluish gray T-shirt off the hanger. Something about Samantha pulled at his natural instincts to nurture. He remembered the sullen little girl who looked at the world from the outskirts. She was skittish and unsure—almost afraid. Behind her brassy persona he saw glimpses of that same fear, and he wondered what she was running from.

He whipped up a few breakfast sandwiches and grabbed a yogurt from the refrigerator before he walked over to her cabin.

She answered the door wearing yoga pants, a long shirt and a smile. "Come in, I have to grab my watermelon lip gloss." She looked over her shoulder as she walked away. All he could think about was making sure she had to apply that all day long.

"I brought you breakfast." He walked in and stood next to the doorway.

She returned holding the tube of gloss in the air. "Still trying to fatten me up?"

He shook his head. "No. Eating in front of you would be rude, so I brought you food." Truth was he wanted to fatten her up. She was beyond underweight, but he could see she was fit and seemed healthy. He pulled one sandwich from his coat pocket. He unwrapped it and took a bite. Nothing went together better than bread, cheese, eggs and bacon.

"You got one of those for me?" She moved toward him like a bug to a light.

He teased her. He took another bite and slowly chewed before he swallowed. All the while, she watched the bacon peeking past the sourdough bread. "I brought you a yogurt. Seemed more your thing." He reached into his right pocket for the strawberry yogurt.

She deflated in front of him like a punctured raft. "Oh, yes, that's probably a better choice." She reached forward to take what he offered.

He held it out of her reach. "Or ... you could have what's behind door number two."

Her chin lifted, and her eyes sparkled with interest. "Ooh ... I'm intrigued."

"Are you now?" With food in both hands, he lifted them into the air. "Tell me, what intrigues you?"

She looked him up and down like he was a tasty meal and for a minute he wished he were.

"Everything. I want everything." She sounded so excited and happy. He would have a hard time denying her.

"Let's start with breakfast." He walked into her kitchen and set the yogurt on the table before he pulled the other sandwich from his pocket and offered it to her.

"I think I may love you already." She unwrapped it and took a bite. The humming sounds of satisfaction she made sent his heart racing and body parts pulsing. So as not to embarrass himself by the swell in his jeans, he turned around and opened the door.

"We should go." The cold air hit, and any evidence of his desire disappeared. "It's chilly, so grab a jacket." He zipped his up to his chin. Yesterday was hot. Today was cold. Weather was as confusing as women.

Dalton led her to his truck where he opened her door and helped her inside. When she raised the sandwich to take a bite, he took one instead.

"Hey, that's mine." She pulled it aside like it was something to be treasured. Something more than a simple egg sandwich.

"We can share." He'd finished his in four bites. Hers looked better, but maybe that was because she looked at it like she looked at him—with hungry eyes. He shut the door and made his way to the driver's side.

By the time he buckled in, she turned in her seat to face him. "You want more of what I got?"

One thing Samantha was good at was the art of double entendre.

"What are you offering?" After last night's kiss and the declaration that she was leaving, Dalton wasn't sure how to proceed. He didn't know how to do short-term unless it was *really* short-term, like one night. Before incarceration, he had a long-term girlfriend. Casey had been at the bar that fateful night. She'd stuck with him through the trial, but as soon as he went away, so did she. On their final visit, she said his reputation would ruin her. He knew that to be true. No one would give him the chance to prove he was something other than a killer.

He'd decided then to be a hit-it-and-quit-it guy, but Samantha seemed different. Outside she gave the impression of a good-time girl, but her kisses weren't those of a woman who practiced hit and run.

There was an innocence and awe about the way she responded to him. Like she'd never been truly kissed in her life. That made him think ... just maybe he could risk more with her. Until she said she couldn't keep him.

They sat in front of the fire last night. Everyone paired up except Doc, who'd remained single since his wife's death. Dalton didn't want to be like him, old and alone. His friends were blissfully happy and moving forward with their lives. He wanted that for himself, but he didn't know how to get it. He was on pause.

"Where do you need to stop today?" he asked as he backed out of the driveway.

"We can stop where I need to go too?" She said it like it was a shock. "I thought we were running your errands."

"Doesn't mean we can't run yours too. What do you need?"

She rolled those pretty dark eyes. "The real question is, what *don't* I need?"

"All right. Let's phrase it this way. What do you want?" He knew what he wanted. He wanted her. In his head, it made sense. They could have fun while she was here. His heart knew better. He finished one kiss and wanted the next. She was like that extra piece of pie you wanted but knew you shouldn't have because there was no stopping once you tasted it.

"I want a television. I want groceries. I want a new cell phone."

"All right. That helps with logistics. We'll hit the phone store first, then the electronics store. I'd love to take you to lunch at my favorite burger place, and then we'll grocery shop before we head back to Aspen Cove. Sound good?"

"Perfect. Grocery shopping was all you had on your list?"

"And lunch."

"It's always food with you."

"Not always." He turned the radio on. "But I like to taste things." He risked a quick glance at her. "How much lip gloss did you bring?"

Her wide smile told him she had plenty. She wet her lips with a single lick. It was sexy and seductive and super hot because Dalton knew she wasn't trying. She was responding to her base instincts. Samantha didn't have to try. She was stunning. He liked women who didn't require much maintenance. Samantha was that girl. She could wear a trash bag cinched at the waist and make it look good.

A song played on the radio he recognized. It had the same rhythm as the music Samantha played that night on the beach.

"You were playing this song."

Out of the corner of his eye, he could see her nod. "I like it."

"Do you know the lyrics?"

She laughed. "By heart." She fidgeted in her seat and pulled at the belt across her chest. "It's a song about looking like you have it all but knowing inside you're hollow."

"Sounds grim." He didn't know what it looked like to have it all, but he sure knew what hollow felt like. It felt like six years in prison. Coming home to find that life went on without you was brutal.

"No, not so much grim as honest. I think we all hide behind the truth that people make for us. It may not be the truth as we see it for ourselves."

He thought about that for a few minutes. He knew how people viewed him. He also knew he wasn't that man. "Yes, but once you're labeled, it's often who you become."

She nodded. "A shame, really, because I think we are so much more as a whole than as the various parts people focus on."

He knew he liked her, but that statement confirmed it. "What do you think is worse, lying to yourself about who you are, or lying to others?" He'd spent the last year telling himself he was fine being an island. He didn't need anything but his job or anyone other than his friends and family. Those were lies. He'd had dreams that were dashed by a dose of gallantry.

She turned her body to face him and leaned against the door. "I think we all lie to ourselves, and in lying to ourselves, we lie to others. Don't let your lie become your truth." She hummed along with the song until the music faded into the next.

"You have a beautiful voice. Have you considered a career in music?"

She laughed until she choked. "Sure, it's crossed my mind."

"You laugh, but you are good." She had a voice like a lover's caress. He could listen to her serenade him all day. "Seriously, sing me something."

"You want me to sing you a song?" She reached into her pocket and slicked on more gloss, which only made his mouth water for another kiss. "What song?"

"Whatever, but I love the oldies." He could picture her singing anything from Stevie Nicks to Aretha.

She leaned forward and changed the radio station until it landed on his favorite music channel. When the Lynyrd Skynyrd song "Freebird" played, and she belted out the lyrics like she'd written them. He was a goner.

"Wow."

"I can't do the original justice, but what a great song. Kind of sad when you think about the lyrics. It's about a man explaining to a woman why he can't settle down and make a commitment. He has to let her go."

He hated to ask, but he needed to know. "Speaking of leaving, how long do you plan to stay?"

"As long as I can. Work can be demanding and unpredictable."

"Do you love what you do?" He turned onto the highway that led to Copper Creek.

She pulled her upper lip between her teeth. Over the last few days, he'd seen her do that when the question was tough.

"I love many aspects about my job. I dislike others, but isn't that the nature of work? Some days are good. Some days are bad. Do you like your job every day?"

He did. He loved to cook, but cooking at Maisey's wasn't the dream. "I love what I do."

"Lucky you. You're living the dream."

"I didn't say that. I said I love what I do, but cooking in my mom's diner wasn't the dream." He gripped the steering wheel until he felt the texture of the leather on his palms.

"So, what was the dream, and why aren't you going after it?"

"It's complicated." He gave her a quick glance and saw the softness and acceptance in her expression. Would she be that accepting if she learned the truth? He didn't want to find out. She was leaving, so the truth didn't matter. "I wanted to open a culinary school."

"So why don't you?"

It all sounded so easy when she said it, but it wasn't easy. "I never finished school. I was about to when I got into some legal trouble." He waited for her to ask for more details, but she didn't.

"You can still finish." Her voice lifted in excitement. "What's stopping you?"

Her excitement bled into him. "You're right. I could. I'll give it some thought. I've got stuff to take care of first." Prison gobbled up the best years of his life. The years he could have used to make a name for himself. Who wanted to learn to cook from a guy who spent more time in a penitentiary than a kitchen?

Conversation ate up the rest of the trip, and before he knew it, they were pulling into a place where she could get a phone and a television.

When the salesperson offered to back up the old phone to the new phone, she said she wanted a new number. She said it with such desperation that Dalton was sure Samantha had secrets too.

CHAPTER TEN

The whole point of getting a new phone was so she wouldn't have to see the sheer number of missed calls and emails from her agent and manager, not to mention auxiliary staff and the few reporters she knew well.

Turns out that walking into a crowd after a concert and disappearing wasn't the way to lie low. Indigo was the new *Where's Waldo*.

With a phone in hand, she followed Dalton to where televisions lined the walls.

"If you were trying to hide, you could have gotten a burner phone. It would have cost less than setting up a new account."

Her heart hammered in her chest. Hiding was the objective, but she hadn't realized she'd been so transparent with her actions.

"I'm separating work from my personal life. I've been here for a few days, and my phone has been on fire with a work-related crisis." The crisis being her disappearance. No less than fifty calls and emails had been flooding her phone daily.

Desperate measures were propelled by desperation. At the risk of losing herself completely, she needed time to let herself settle back into a normal life. Getting a phone where the only people to call were vetted was part of the process.

With her brown hair and toned-down clothes, she hoped to blend in. After one glance around the electronics superstore, she realized no one paid her any mind. Maybe she considered herself more important than she was.

"They say size matters." Dalton looked at her with a devilish grin. "How big do you like yours?"

She held in the laughter and played along. At the end were the small screens. She stopped and stared at the monitors no bigger than a laptop.

"This one lacks length and girth. While it would do the job, it doesn't impress me. I fear the experience would be unsatisfying."

Dalton barely controlled his laughter. His shoulders shook as she followed him down the row.

"What about this?" He pointed to a wide screen television. One that was long and narrow.

She stood in front of it and analyzed the proportions. "Do you really think length is more important than width?"

He rubbed his finely trimmed beard with his calloused hands. The scruffy sound filled in the surrounding silence. "This size makes sure in the long run you don't miss an inch of what's there. Having said that, I imagine having a balance between the two is more important." He moved all the way to the end, where eighty inches hung on the wall in front of them. "Now this is a beast. It's got it all."

Samantha looked at Dalton. As much as she tried to keep her eyes on his face, they rolled down his body.

Tension skirted through her the second they talked length and girth. It appeared he wasn't unaffected either. Hanging toward the right between his legs was the growing evidence. If Dalton Black had been a television, he would have been a high-definition big screen.

She cleared her head and looked at the beast hanging on the wall in front of her. "That would never fit."

He moved behind her and rested his chin on the top of her head.

She wanted to lean back into his body but was afraid she'd be poked by his specifications.

"You can always make room for what you desire." He left her in front of the massive television with her mouth hanging open. Were they still talking about TVs? Had they ever been talking about TVs?

She couldn't deny they shared a mutual attraction. She knew it before the first kiss. Hell, she knew it when she was twelve. He was like a live wire that skirted over her skin.

Hot.

Tingling.

Powerful.

When she got to where he stood in front of another large unit, she said, "I have little experience with this kind of thing." Again, not talking about televisions. "I'm used to the standard size you find in hotels and such."

He turned to face her. "You don't want to settle for small. You'll walk away feeling disappointed."

"I get that, but if it's too big, I may not walk at all." She grabbed the salesman and asked him to ring up the size in the middle.

At the register, the cashier told her she owed $1842.36. She pulled out a brick of twenties wrapped with a purple band.

"Cash?" Dalton asked. The scar above his eye lifted.

She stared at him and smiled. "It's easier to use." She paid, and they took her purchases to the truck.

He helped her inside. While he rounded the front of the truck, she texted Deanna and her mother the new phone number.

"You hungry?"

"Starved." Who knew electronics could give her such an appetite?

Ten minutes later, they pulled in front of a little hole-in-the-wall diner called Chachi's. It was modeled after the sitcom *Happy Days*. He raced around to help her out. She loved how he could be so chivalrous and yet not. His talk was anything but gentlemanly, but he treated her like she mattered. Not as a means to influence his portfolio, but as a human. Her value wasn't dependent on her net worth. He seemed to appreciate her for who she was in that moment.

"My treat," Samantha said. She took the seat in the far booth where she could see everything around her. She was feeling brazen and brave having made it through a store without the slightest nod of recognition.

"You're not paying. I don't care how many bricks of cash are in your purse. I pay for my date."

She felt giddy inside. "So exciting." She'd never been on an actual date. She'd ordered room service and watched movies on pay-per-view, but all of those 'dates' ended up on her hotel tab.

"You're easy."

She giggled. "Yes, but not cheap." She took the menu from the stand and looked over the offerings. She would be easy and cheap since the most expensive item on the menu was under ten bucks. "What do you recommend?"

"You want me to order for you?" He slid the menu from her hands and turned it to face him. "You trust me?"

She trusted him, which was odd because she didn't trust most men. "It's food. You're a chef. I trust you."

When he smiled, she knew her trust in him was important.

A young male waiter named Todd came over and stood in front of them. He looked at Dalton, then at her, but his eyes focused on her. He stared for what seemed like an eternity before a grin took over his face.

"You're—"

"Starving." She hoped that line hadn't lost its magic. It worked at the bakery, and she prayed it would work here.

Todd nodded his head and pulled a pen from behind his ear. "What would you like?"

Samantha looked to Dalton who cleared his throat to get the waiter's attention. "The lady will have the Joanie, and I'll have The Fonz. We'll share a plate of Happy Fries. Bring us two chocolate malts."

Todd scribbled the order down and took one last long look at Samantha before he left.

She knew she'd been recognized but hoped he'd respect her privacy. She was on a date and didn't want it ruined.

"You shouldn't be carrying so much cash around. Purple bands means two grand. People get mugged for less."

"How would you know what a purple band holds? Are you a numismatist?"

His long arms had no problem reaching across the table to hold her hands. His thumbs brushed over her knuckles. "No, I like money but not enough to collect it or study it. I had a roommate who knew a lot about how the banks bundled money. Talked about it all the time." He ran his thumbs across her unadorned fingers. She'd never worn a ring. Had never been one for much jewelry.

The day her mom pawned her wedding ring to get food, Samantha promised herself she wouldn't let a ring grace her fingers until she was one hundred percent certain about the giver. It was an unrealistic expectation because it was impossible to be one hundred percent sure about anything or anyone.

"Yeah, money is good to have when you need things, but it's not the panacea for the world's problems."

"If you had the solution to the world's problems, you wouldn't need money. You'd be filthy rich."

"Is that what you want? To be filthy rich?" She liked that she could sit with a man who had no idea of her worth. At the last tally, it was over a one hundred and twenty million. It wasn't like she had that much money in the bank, but her talent was bankable. She had enough that she wouldn't have to work again. It wasn't her future she worried about these days. Lots of people depended on her. Her mother and dozens of employees would suffer without her. It was their future that kept her on stage.

"I'm not motivated by money," Dalton said as the waiter delivered everything they ordered at once. He picked up a fry drenched in a cheesy meat sauce. "I'm motivated by food." He looked at Todd, who stood staring at Samantha. "We're good," he said and waited for the waiter to walk away before he looked directly at her with those beautiful steel blue eyes. "Oh, and kisses. Not any kisses though. I particularly like yours."

She lifted the top bun to see what was hiding beneath. Turns out, the Joanie burger was a fully loaded cardiac arrest waiting to happen. Massive patty, covered in cheese, bacon, grilled mushrooms, and green chili. She wasn't sure she'd be able to get it into her mouth. Then she remembered what Dalton said in the electronics store. *"You can always make room for what you desire."* She wanted it all.

When Todd came back to collect their plates, he stared once more. "I like your hair."

Dalton lifted his palms in the air. "Dude, are you trying to be annoying, or does it come naturally for you?"

He gave Dalton a look that could kill, and then he addressed Samantha. "I see why you'd need protection, but surely you can afford someone with better manners."

Dalton's fingers folded into fists. She wasn't sure what he'd do if Todd continued. Didn't want to find out.

"You have a phone?" she asked. "I'm not who you think I am, but what the hell. I get mistaken for her a lot." She moved out of the booth and stood next to Todd who pulled his phone from his apron pocket and lifted it for a selfie.

"Who does he think you are?" Dalton asked.

Samantha waved his question away with a flick of her wrist and stood next to Todd. She put her standard peace sign in front of her chest and smiled. On tiptoes, she kissed his cheek while he snapped the picture.

"I'm a huge fan. Like, obsessive."

"I'm sure she appreciates it." Samantha turned so Dalton couldn't see the wink she gave Todd. "Have a great day. Be cool."

"Ready?" Dalton startled her with his voice whispering in her ear.

"I am."

When they were both in the truck, he asked, "Does that happen a lot?"

She sighed. "More than you could imagine."

Their next stop was Walmart. Samantha hadn't been in one since she was a kid, but they were perfect because it was a one-stop shopping experience. Hell, she could have bought her phone and television here as well. Then again, it might not have been as much fun.

"What do you need?" she asked him.

"Food for an overnighter times two."

"You're leaving?"

"I'll be close. Bowie, Cannon, and I will do some ice fishing tonight and tomorrow before it gets too warm. We like to fish the cove."

"I'm kind of sad that you won't be around. You're like my guilty pleasure."

"You haven't seen pleasure yet." He picked up a bag of oranges and a bunch of bananas.

"Like you, I like our kisses a lot." She lowered her head to hide the blush of truth.

He pushed forward, and then waited for her to catch up. "That's only the beginning, but here's the problem. You're leaving, and that means we probably have to skip the in-between. And I kind of like the in-between."

She pushed her cart down the aisle and tossed in various varieties of fruit, from grapes to apples. *This shopping stuff is awesome.*

"Can't we go with it and see where it leads?"

He left his cart alone and sidled up next to her so his body touched hers on one side. "You already know where this will lead. The question is, how long will it take for us to get there?"

"Since you're leaving, at least two days."

He nuzzled his beard into the crook of her neck. It felt deliciously good.

She ducked away from his touch. It was too ticklish and tantalizing. She wanted him in a place where she could savor every whisker that brushed against her skin.

"We haven't hit the third date yet. You know there's a third-date rule. Besides, outside of breakfast, I'm not sure you can cook. I haven't seen it yet."

"I'll show you my skills, but you'll have to wait until I get back."

"It will be so hard." She emphasized the last word.

He groaned. "You have no idea."

She raced ahead, tossing whatever looked good in her basket. If she couldn't have him, she'd have chocolate and cake and chocolate and pie and chocolate.

CHAPTER ELEVEN

What the hell was he doing? Dalton popped the cap off another beer and stared across the lake to the cabin next door to his. Shadows in her window caught his attention.

"What's she like?" Cannon asked.

"She's nice." He took a deep drink and savored the bubbling burn as it moved down his throat. *She was nice. Nice to look at. Nice to be with. Nice to talk to. Nice to kiss.*

"Is this already a thing between you two?" Bowie pulled up a chair and sat next to Dalton.

It seemed funny they were sitting on a sheet of ice in the middle of a lake, but that's where they were. How crazy was it that he left a woman happy to share her warm cabin—and most likely her bed—for the company of two dudes, a six-pack of beer, and a case of frostbite?

"Are we a thing? I don't even know what that is. Do I like her? Yes. Is it going to get serious? No. She's leaving." His voice sank on the last word.

"You say that like it bothers you." Cannon tossed a piece of cardboard onto the ice and sat on top of it. "She *says* she's leaving, but so did Sage. That woman had nothing but an exit plan when she arrived. Maybe you can change Samantha's mind."

"You're forgetting the details. Sage was unemployed. Samantha owns a PR company or runs it or works there. I don't know exactly. All I know, is her life isn't here in Aspen Cove."

"You kiss her?" Now it was Bowie's turn to ask the stupid questions.

"What am I, fifteen? I don't need a year to get to first base." He'd rushed straight for first, but held off stealing second and beyond.

The brothers looked at each other. "I guess that's a yes," Cannon said. "Since you're our brother and all, we're looking out for you."

He cut them a sharp look that dared them to argue. "Like you did for each other? No, thanks. One of you went from monk to married. And you," he pointed to Cannon, "are running to catch up."

"Don't knock it until you try it," Bowie answered.

"Not happening." He'd given it a lot of thought over the last year. He'd seen the faces of the women who heard about his past. One moment they were sharing a beer, the next he watched their taillights fade into the distance, never to be heard from again. "Marriage. It's not for everyone." Newlyweds surrounded Dalton. Like a bad case of the flu, no one in Aspen Cove seemed to be immune. "Can't believe my mom ran to the altar again. I never thought that would happen—and not with Ben. Your dad is great, but he has an ugly temper."

Cannon laughed and then slapped his hand over his mouth. "He only has an ugly temper when he drinks, which he no longer does. He's never hit a woman until Sage, and that was an accident."

Dalton cringed at the memory of that day when both Cannon and Sage showed up to Bea's funeral sporting black eyes. "Still, most people don't forgive and forget, but my mom did." He hoped he could get there someday. He craved the day when he could look at any person and see the good in them without trying to figure out their angle first. He wanted a day to come when people could see him for who he was, not the crime he committed.

Bowie nodded his head while an "Ahh ..." left his mouth. "Samantha doesn't know about your incarceration."

"No, and I'm not telling her. If she were staying, it would be a different matter, but she's not. It's not like I'm Charles Manson and get off on killing people. It was a one-time event." He considered Lucy's advice and spoke it out loud. "I'm not going to strip down and blurt out I have herpes."

Bowie leaned back too far, and his chair tumbled, sending him to the ice. He scrambled up. "You what? Who the hell gave you herpes?"

Dalton let out a growl that could frighten a bear. "I don't have herpes. It's a figure of speech." He explained the conversation he had with his parole officer.

Cannon shook his head from side to side the whole time. "I definitely would *not* use that one again. If I were a girl, I'd much rather you be a felon than have an STD."

Bowie grabbed another beer. "I don't know. Take the proper precautions, and it's no big deal."

"So is this where I get the brotherly talk on safe sex?" Dalton finished his beer and tossed it into the plastic bag they'd set out for trash. "You know I'm older than you, right?"

Bowie handed him another. "You've got me by a month."

"Still makes me older." He lit the stove they'd set up to cook hot dogs. It wasn't more than a Sterno can on a stand, but it worked. He glanced back to the shore and wondered what Samantha was up to. *What was she doing? What was she eating? Most likely sitting in front of her big screen TV, eating fruit and chocolate, since that was what filled the bulk of her cart.*

"As for safe sex ... no glove, no love, brother," Cannon said with a chuckle.

"Am I going to regret coming fishing?" He popped the top on his beer and listened to the hissing carbonation escape.

They both shrugged and said, "Probably," in unison.

This was the first year in many that any of them had been ice fishing. Dalton's time in prison and the accident that killed Bowie and Cannon's mom and Bowie's fiancée had stalled their lives for years.

At yesterday's bonfire, they decided they had to do it now since the days were getting warmer and the ice would melt soon. They'd already wasted so much time.

Before they settled on a place, they drilled through the ice to make sure they wouldn't end up wet by morning. The cove was always the last place to melt since it sat on the shady side of the lake, surrounded by walls of granite and aspen trees.

"Is it weird?" Dalton turned to Bowie.

"Is what weird?"

In the fading light, he could see Bowie's scowl. He knew that Bowie couldn't hear his thoughts, but Dalton wondered about lots of things. He'd been curious about Katie, her wealth, her heart, and their life together. Most of all, he wondered what it felt like to be a dad.

"Being a dad."

The scowl turned into a smile. "Oh man, you have no idea what it's like to look at a tiny human being and know she's half you."

Cannon slapped Bowie's knee. "The bad half. Sad for you because babies have a no return policy. Good thing she's half Katie, or Sahara would be in trouble."

They took a package of hot dogs from the cooler and speared them onto sticks they'd found.

"You're right. Everything good about Sahara comes from Katie. She'll grow into the bad shit later when I teach her how to fight and protect herself."

Dalton took a swig of his beer. "I'll protect her. It's what I do."

They all sat in silence. "Maybe next time you can pull a different tool out of your box other than the fist of death," Cannon said.

Dalton raised his right hand into the air. "But it's so effective." No one could argue with that.

How many women had cried over the death of Andy Kranz? How many let out a sigh of relief? How many wouldn't have to find out something sinister lay under his smile because Dalton had killed him?

Bowie rotated his hot dog over the fire and glanced toward the shore.

Dalton could tell a part of him wanted to race across the lake to get back home to Katie and his daughter.

Bowie sat up tall. "You know what I can't wait for?" He reached for a bun to cradle his charred dog. "I can't wait to hear her first laugh." He took a bite.

"Will that be soon?" Dalton knew nothing about babies. He knew they ate and pooped and slept. That was the extent of his knowledge.

"The book says it happens around three months. We'll see."

Dalton sat forward and took his dog from the flame. It was perfect, not charred like Bowie's, or undercooked like Cannon's. His was hot, sweating, and juicy.

"They come with a manual? When did that happen?" He squeezed a line of mustard on each side of the meat and took a bite. A good hot dog was almost as satisfying as a good kiss. Almost. He stared back to Samantha's cabin. *I'm such an idiot.*

"They have this book called *What To Expect The First Year.*"

"Sounds like a riveting read." Dalton continued to stare across the lake.

Cannon kicked at Bowie. "This asshole read the first tome too. It's called *What To Expect When You're Expecting.* I opened it up and took a peek. Made me want to tuck my Johnson away forever."

Bowie eyed Cannon with a marksman stare. "You're next, unless big brother over here knocks up number seven."

Dalton choked on his food. "Number seven? I've never hit the target. No babies under my belt."

Cannon impaled another hot dog onto a stick and let it sit on the flame. It took time for the small fire to cook, but building a blaze on ice wasn't recommended. "I wouldn't put *can't hit the target* on your resume either. He was talking about her address. Samantha lives at 7 Lake Circle."

"No, don't reduce her to a number. She's Samantha White." If she were getting a nickname, he'd be the one to give it to her.

"Hard to believe she used to live here." Cannon kicked back and lay on the ice facing the darkening sky. Thousands of stars flickered above them. The moon cast a glow across the white surface. A beacon leading to her door.

"I remember her mom," Bowie said. "She was a classic battered woman. I came up behind her in the Corner Store, and she knocked over three displays trying to distance herself from me. I didn't recognize it then, but in hindsight I see it now. I was big, and she was scared."

Anger coiled inside Dalton. He knew that kind of fear. He'd lived it. His mom had lived it. Now he knew Samantha had lived it. She was more than the little girl from Aspen Cove who did well. She was a survivor. She was strong. He was weak because he wouldn't survive another minute without her kiss.

CHAPTER TWELVE

Nothing cured a lonely heart better than Ben & Jerry's Chunky Monkey ice cream and binge watching *Supernatural*. It probably wasn't the best idea to watch a show about angels, demons, and any other nightmare an active imagination could conjure while being alone in a cabin on a lake, but after the first two episodes, she was hooked.

In between ice cream, candy, and an apple as her healthy addition, she peeked out the window across the lake and wondered which of the small fires glowing in the darkness was Dalton's. Shadows played with her mind and imagination. Every once in a while, she swore she heard footsteps on her deck or a knock at her door. Each time she looked, there was no one and nothing but the sway of pine branches and the whisper of the wind racing between the cabins.

Though she'd slept alone in the house since she arrived, knowing Dalton was next door comforted her. That sense of comfort now sat somewhere on the frozen lake. Thoughts of him had invaded her dreams since that first night. How could they not? He kissed like a rock star still trying to impress groupies.

Tonight, the memory of his kisses wouldn't go away. Maybe it was because he planted the seed of more to come. His words about knowing where this would end made every cell in her body spark with hope that he'd be right.

As she pressed play for season one, episode nine, the thump of heavy footsteps sounded on her porch. Her heart leaped inside her chest. Maybe those shadows in the dark weren't her imagination after all.

Had her manager found her? The press? What if it was some evil entity she conjured by watching episode after episode of a show where demonic intentions ruled the day? She looked around the cabin for a weapon, but all she had was a bag of miniature candy bars and a half-finished pint of ice cream.

A soft tap on the door had her moving forward in her stockinged feet. She crept silently forward hoping she wouldn't be heard. Maybe she could ignore whoever was there, and they would go away. When she dared to look through the peephole, her heart nearly exploded. Dalton stood on her doorstep. His hair mussed. His cheeks rosy. Sexy as ever. No way she could, or would, ignore him. He was here for more.

She swung the door wide and threw herself at him.

"Hey, good to see you too." He wrapped his arms around her until they were glued chest-to-chest. He shuffled both their bodies through the doorway and closed it behind them. "I missed you too."

"You did?" She pressed tighter into his hold, not wanting to pull her face from his chest. He smelled so earthy and manly. One deep inhale and the scent of him filled her. He was citrus and pine and campfire with a hint of hot dog.

"Yes, I did." He brushed his lips to the top of her head. "I can't get you out of my mind."

"Do you want to?"

He placed his hands gently at her waist and lifted. Instinctively, she wrapped her legs around him, feeling his desire press between her thighs. If that fire didn't ignite her flame, she didn't know what would.

They were body-to-body and now mouth-to-mouth as he kissed her with such intensity, she thought she'd implode. His tongue slipped between her lips, causing her to melt in his arms. He made love to her mouth, giving her a taste of what it would be like when he made love to her body. Energy passed between them, raw, hungry, and carnal.

With her glued to him, he walked her to the couch and fell onto the soft leather, pulling her down but not once breaking the kiss. His hands explored her body, first over her shirt until he found his way beneath it. His rough, calloused fingertips left a blazing trail of desire wherever he touched.

Seconds turned into minutes as they enjoyed the feel and flavor of each other. A shift of her body pressed her into his hardness. The firmness she felt told her they were pressing hard and fast toward more.

There were so many things she should tell him before they crossed that threshold. She pulled back, heaving for breath.

"Dalton, there are things you should know about me." While her mind told her to wait, her fingers pulled down the zipper of his jacket. His help was appreciated when he yanked the coat off and tossed it into the corner. She ran her fingers over the cotton covered, rippling muscles of his chest.

Quick as a flash, his hands moved under her shirt to her bare belly and grazed her heated skin from waistband to breasts. He stopped at the edge of her bra.

"Are you married?" his deep voice murmured.

"What?" It was so hard to think when his fingers skimmed under the lace. "No."

"Engaged?" He brushed his thumbs across the soft material.
"No."

"Then I don't care," he growled. "All I care about is this thing burning between us."

"There are things you should know."

He sat up until she straddled his lap and their chests touched.

Her pebbled nipples sent code to her core, which sent the message of *shut up* to her brain.

He quirked a sexy brow at her. "You want to exchange resumes?" He ran his lips over her collarbone, biting down with enough force to make her gasp. "There are things you should know about me too. You want me to stop kissing you to tell you?"

Hell no, her inner voice screamed.

"Are you married?" she teased. Her hand slipped beneath the cotton of his shirt to feel the heat of his skin.

He nipped at the sensitive area that sat between her neck and shoulder. "Not married, not engaged. Tonight, I'm yours ... if you want me." His breathy reply sent shivers racing across her body. His hands dipped past her waistband and caressed her bottom.

She was done. There was nothing he could say to change her mind. He was Dalton Black, her first crush. She would have him, and she would enjoy him.

"I've got a bed."

He chuckled. "Do you now? I'd love to see it." He was beastly strong. He twisted his body so his feet hit the floor, but hers stayed glued to his.

With his hands still inside her pants, he said, "You have the nicest ass." He grabbed handfuls of it and rose while Samantha held on for the ride. He stepped between the coffee table and couch and made his way to her room.

She expected him to toss her onto the bed. Her experience was, once a bed came into play, everything went quickly from that point forward. Dalton surprised her when he lowered her gently to the edge.

Steel blue eyes once hard were now like molten glass that held a sizzling, electric heat. Although she wore an oversized shirt and leggings, he looked at her as if she wore sexy lingerie or—better yet—nothing at all.

Hungry eyes took her in, from her high ponytail to her fuzzy socks. "You're so beautiful."

She tried to stand, but he shook his head. "Let me look at you for a minute."

While he stared at her, she drank him in. He wore a colored T-shirt that would become her favorite because the silver blue of it brought out the passion in his eyes. The material stretched across his broad chest. Mountains of muscle rippled to a narrow waist. Jeans that fit him perfectly hung low on his hips and hugged thighs she knew were honed from stone.

He could take all the minutes he wanted because the view was damn fine from where she sat.

"I thought you were staying the night on the ice." Her voice barely registered above a whisper.

"That was my plan, but every time I looked across the lake and saw the light on, I knew this was where I wanted to be."

"What about your brothers?" She inched back on the bed until her entire body rested on the soft mattress.

"They're men. They get it." He bent forward to unlace his boots. Once he toed them off, he climbed onto the bed beside her. The mattress dipped under his weight, making her roll toward him. She didn't fight it. She loved the feel of being next to him. He was so large. She was so small. Together, they were perfect.

"We're breaking the third-date rule," she said.

He splayed his hand across her stomach and pressed her to the mattress. "I don't like rules."

As his palm inched up to cup her breasts, she let out a sigh. It had been so long since anyone had touched her. She nearly wept with joy.

"Our rules, our way." She pulled the hem of her shirt over her head and threw it aside. Dalton groaned at the sight of her. One good thing about having money was being able to afford nice under-things. The black lace bra was made from the finest, softest material. Though her breasts were small, his palm seemed to like the weight.

"So pretty." He leaned down and breathed heat over one tight, aching nipple. Her back arched, forcing the lacy cup against his lips.

"There's no hurry. We've got all night." He left one breast and moved to the other to repeat his hot, tortuous tease.

Being all about equality, Samantha tugged at the hem of his shirt until it bunched around his chest. "I want to see you. I want to taste you."

A slow, sexy rumble vibrated through the air. Dalton reached behind him, grabbing a handful of cotton and pulling it forward and over his head.

She tugged it from his arms and lifted it to her nose. "I love the way you smell."

He shrugged. "It's a body wash Abby makes."

"Abby?" She had no idea who that was, but a thread of jealousy twisted inside her. "Who's Abby?"

"Is that jealousy in those pretty eyes?" He lifted his body and straddled her hips.

The heavy hardness of him rubbed against her, the friction was better than anything she'd felt in ages.

"No, I don't have a right to be jealous." She bit her lip, thinking about Abby and conjuring all sorts of images. Pretty blondes. Dynamic redheads. Tatted up biker chicks. She released a telling sigh. "All right. I'm a little jealous. This is my first time with you, and I don't want to share you with anyone else."

With his palms flat against her body, he caressed her skin with long, soft strokes. "There's no one here but us. Abby Garrett is a local woman who raises bees and makes soaps and stuff. It's only you and me." His hands floated over her skin. A shiver of pleasure raced through her cells, slamming straight to her core.

She sucked in a cleansing breath, trying to settle her nerves. It was sex. She'd done it before, but somehow this was different. Dalton wasn't stripping down or impatient for her to do the same. He was enjoying every second.

Rather than rush through the mechanics of joining their two bodies, Samantha got in touch with the emotions she was feeling.

Fear.

Passion.

Excitement.

Anticipation.

Love.

The last one floored her. *I don't love Dalton.* She loved the way he made her feel.

No matter where he touched—her stomach, her hair, her arms, her face—the needy ache inside her grew. Her body was already humming, and they'd barely begun.

"God, I still have my pants on, and I'm close to being finished," she panted.

He chuckled. "We're only beginning."

She traced the lines of his tattoos. "Boston? When were you there?"

A smirk of a smile graced his face. "Not the city. The band."

She needed the distraction of conversation, or she'd erupt in seconds. "You had the name of a band tattooed on your arm?" She wondered if some poor fool was sporting the name Indigo on their body.

"Bad decision. Too much alcohol." He fell forward, catching himself on his arms. While one held his weight, the other snaked around her back to unhook her bra. Dalton was dexterous—one try, and it was loose. But he didn't strip it from her in one quick movement. He peeled it from her body inch by inch. She was a gift he unwrapped, revealing the treasure slowly.

Her nipples were hard and painfully tight. His lips covered one, and the heat of his mouth sucked it in. She no longer felt the tingling discomfort. It was replaced with the most amazing sensation created by his superior oral skills. A frenzied fire that raced through her body.

Her hips pumped against him, trying to find the release she craved.

"In such a hurry," he said. His lips touched her breast. The vibration of his words coursed through her. "Don't rush to the end when the middle is so much fun."

Dalton showed her how much enjoyment floating in the middle could bring. He spent minutes raking his whiskers over her breasts. Little nips and sucks added in between for her pleasure. He moved down to make love to her belly button with his tongue. Who knew that she would quiver and shake so hard? He leaned back and put his thumbs into the waistband of her pants and tugged, stripping her naked. She was grateful for the distance from his tongue, and yet she couldn't wait until it returned to torture her again.

Her labored breath slowed as the cool air rushed over her skin. She was on fire, and all she wore were fuzzy socks. Scratch that, Dalton pulled those off with his teeth and climbed up her naked body.

"Feel good?" His hands were back on her. They seemed to be everywhere. His lips and tongue teased her from her collarbone to what he'd referred to as her anvil-sharp hips.

"Be careful. I'd hate for you to poke an eye out." She ran her fingers through his hair and followed his movements down.

He looked up at her with hunger. "Heading for softer ground." His large hands rested on her legs to open them wide—wide enough for his shoulders to fit between the cradle of her thighs. Good thing she was limber. All thoughts of being a contortionist ended when the heat of his mouth and the scruff of his beard made contact. The rough hair on his jawline scratched her delicate skin and left a delicious burn in its wake.

She'd been a taut string—a coiled mass of energy ready to spike at any moment. She never expected to come undone so fast and so furiously. He stroked her with the velvet of his tongue. Suckled her with his lips and hummed his satisfaction at her taste. She climbed higher and higher until the sensation tore through her. Dalton stayed with her for every glorious, pulsating moment.

Not to be rushed, he kept her quivering and moaning and praying for it to end and continue at the same time. When she lay next to him, wiped out and limp, he pulled her into his arms and held her tightly to his chest. He hugged her like she was important. Like she mattered.

"How is it that I've had the best sex of my life and you aren't even naked?" She stroked his dark, hair-dusted chest and followed the trail to his pants, where his quick reflexes stopped her progress.

"Sweetheart. That wasn't sex. That was foreplay."

"Oh holy hell."

He climbed off the bed. She was too weak to move. By the light of the hallway, she watched him walk away and return with a glass of water and a bowl of grapes.

He dropped his pants but not his boxers and climbed into bed beside her. She drank the water and shared a few grapes before she turned to him.

"Your turn." She covered her yawn and then dropped her hands to his magnificent chest. Her fingers touched every ridge of muscle until he threaded his fingers through hers and pulled them to his mouth for a kiss.

"I'm not keeping tabs. We've got more than tonight. We have all the nights until you leave."

After the best experience in her existence, she wasn't sure leaving would be possible. How could a woman walk away from his talents—his tongue?

He reached over her and turned out the light, then scooted down next to her and pulled her close to his body. She'd never felt more cherished in her life. This was special. He gave more than he took. She felt happy. She felt satisfied. She felt loved.

CHAPTER THIRTEEN

Best night of his damn life, and he didn't even get laid.

The sun hadn't risen when Dalton trudged across the lake toward Bowie and Cannon with a pound of bacon and a dozen eggs tucked under his arm. He figured since he chose babe over brothers, he owed them something. Maybe a hot breakfast would reduce the variety of ways they would call him "whipped".

A layer of frost crackled beneath his boots while his breath turned to fog. What were they thinking when they planned to stay on the lake for two nights? *Idiots.*

Another decision made after too many beers. Definitely a chest-pounding Neanderthal moment of increased testosterone.

Holding Samantha in his arms all night would be worth the razzing he'd get all day. Hell, it was hard to leave her. Double hell because he was hard all night, but something told him that Samantha gave more than she received, and he wanted to let her know how it felt to be cherished.

He'd walked longer than expected and stopped to look around. He backtracked across the ice, certain he hadn't passed camp among the tents dotting the lake. They had been the only group camped at the edge of the cove.

Something melted into the ice caught his attention. It was the piece of hot dog Cannon had tossed at Bowie last night. "I'll be damned."

He spun in a circle. "I'm not the only one whipped," he said out loud.

He turned back and crunched across the ice, hoping he could make it back to Samantha's before she got up. He'd kissed her goodbye and told her he'd be back. His plan was to warm her bed again tonight. *Still the plan.*

He considered their conversation. The one they had in the throes of arousal where they both agreed to keep their secrets. Although Dalton believed relationships should be built on honesty, he was a realist. Samantha made it clear she was leaving. At best, he could see her when she vacationed in Aspen Cove. Given she owned the house for over two years and this was her first visit, he imagined those times would be few.

He made his way back to her cabin, only to realize he was too late. Dressed in sweatpants, sneakers, and a Hollywood T-shirt, she jogged in place, warming up her muscles.

"Going somewhere?" he called from the edge of the lake. He hopped from the thinning ice to the shore. His walk turned into a jog straight toward her. Once there, he set the breakfast fixings on the stairs.

"Yes, Katie wanted to go for a jog around town. Sage and Lydia are joining us."

"I thought you'd still be in bed." He looked at her with disappointment. "Thought I could make you breakfast. You must be hungry after last night." The way her body shook had to have burned off a thousand calories.

She blushed. "All my motivation to stay in the bed got up early and left." She put a hand on his chest, using him for balance, and pulled her right leg up behind her. Grabbing her toes, she gave it a good stretch before switching to the other side. "Besides, my muscles are sore and could use loosening up."

"I could have helped with that."

She pushed against him, making him stumble back a step. "You caused that." She peeked around his body, looking for her group, but they hadn't arrived. "I've never felt anything so intense. It was like the worst muscle spasm in the best way." She lowered her head to hide the new bloom of pink flooding her cheeks.

"And you'll feel it again."

"Not sure I can handle it." She used his body as exercise equipment, gripping his hips and leaning into him for a deep lunge.

Up and down she moved, and it nearly killed him. Her head bobbing near his zipper made the motion appear almost pornographic.

He stroked her cheek, stopping her movements. "You want to try that while we're naked?"

She hopped up. "Oh. My. God. I get near you, and I lose my mind."

"You're not alone." He heard a commotion behind him and knew he had mere minutes before she disappeared into a group of X chromosomes.

"Dinner tonight?"

She hopped on the step so they were face-to-face. "Can't, I hear it's karaoke night at the bar."

Dalton was confused. "Bowie closed the bar while we were fishing."

"And you're not fishing anymore, so it's back open." She pressed a quick kiss to his lips. "Come to the bar tonight. It should be fun. I'd love to hear you sing."

He gripped her hips to keep her there a moment longer.

"Why would I punish you like that when all I want to do is pleasure you?" Not caring that the three women approached like a storm, he pulled Samantha against him and claimed her mouth. If she was leaving him for the day, the least she could do was leave him with a kiss.

When he released her, there was a sigh from behind. He turned to see Sage, Kate, and Lydia standing there. Katie and Sage had big smiles. Lydia looked like she'd eaten something bad. Then again, with the way she reacted to affectionate couples, Dalton didn't imagine things were good in the love department.

"Tonight. Okay?" Samantha said as she rushed past him.

"Yep, I'll pick you up at six."

She hopped into the air like she'd won something special.

He watched her perfect ass jog out of sight. When he glanced at the front of his jeans, he groaned. She left him with more than a kiss. He adjusted his discomfort and picked up the bacon and eggs.

Someone was going to eat his damn breakfast, so he marched next door to Bowie's house and walked inside. Though he knew a compromising situation wouldn't present itself with Katie gone and Bowie left home alone with the baby, he didn't expect to find his friend reduced to goo. On the floor, bench-pressing his daughter was the big man himself.

"Who's Daddy's little girl?" he crooned. "My baby. Little miracle. My treasure. Yes," he grinned at the baby, "that's you."

Dalton leaned against the wall and took it all in. Over the last year, he watched a bitter and angry man turn into marshmallow.

Katie brought peace and purpose to Bowie's life. She kept him on his toes. Who wouldn't want to be a better man when you had a woman worth fighting for?

Bowie had fought for both of them. It was funny because people say love heals everything. He didn't believe that until a little girl was born and her daddy's life changed. There wasn't a day Bowie didn't smile. Not a day he didn't have a positive thing to say to someone.

Dalton even noticed that Bowie's once pronounced limp had disappeared. He figured it was because he walked with purpose, determination and pride. Bowie was surrounded by love.

"You forgot to add 'perfect' and 'princess.'" Dalton walked into the room. "You better get started on that one now. I hear girls like that."

"Katie hated it, so I called her 'Duchess.'"

"And now you call her 'Queen'. Tell me again who's whipped?" He lifted the food he brought. "You hungry?"

Bowie sat up and cradled Sahara in his arms. "I could eat."

Dalton walked to the kitchen where he spent a lot of his youth. He knew it almost as well as his own.

"Call your brother. He might be hungry too."

Ten minutes later, Cannon walked in. "Is that bacon I smell?"

They sat at the small table by the window looking over the lake. "You two gave up last night too?"

Cannon picked up a piece of bacon and laughed. "You were gone less than thirty minutes before we packed up. We left two beautiful women sleeping alone. How stupid was that?" He pressed the entire piece of bacon into his mouth.

Bowie added to Cannon's response. "Yeah, you were walking toward a hot body, and we were looking to freeze our sacks off. Not the smartest move. You get the smart brother prize for the night." He forked a bite of the egg, the yolk dripping to the plate as he held it in front of his mouth. "You get lucky?" He lifted his brows with ridiculous exaggeration.

"Any time I spend with Samantha feels lucky."

Cannon picked up his coffee and took a swig. "No, man, he wants to know if you got laid?"

Something fierce and protective roiled inside him. "Don't talk about her like she's some common girl. She's not. She's more than a lay."

Bowie and Cannon looked at each other and then back to Dalton.

"You got it bad, bro," Bowie said.

"Start saving now," Cannon added, "the ring will set you back big time. If someone hadn't bought that headboard, I'd be in debt for a long time to come."

100

"You can thank Samantha for that. Your headboard is firmly affixed to her bed."

"No shit? Firmly affixed you say? You give it a rocking?" He held his hand up for a high five. "Congrats man."

That didn't sit well with Dalton. He didn't want Bowie and Cannon thinking Samantha was easy.

"We slept."

"Yeah, after you rocked the bed, right?" Bowie wiped up the remaining yolk with the last piece of bacon.

Dalton shook his head. "Nope, we slept. Best damn night of my life. I've never done so little and been so satisfied."

He looked at his new brothers who sat there silent with heads shaking. "He's got it really bad," they said in unison.

CHAPTER FOURTEEN

Samantha's run with the girls was amazing. They rounded the town and headed toward the old paper mill at Samantha's request.

"Heartbreaking to see it empty." She looked into the vacant building. "So many people left when it closed." It nearly broke her heart when her mom came home and told her she'd lost her job.

"Wouldn't it be great if someone could breathe new life into the place?" Katie asked. "What a great project this would be."

Sage wiped at a dusty window and glanced inside. "This would be a huge undertaking. You stick to the park and your family. Leave this to someone else."

Lydia stepped back and looked at the brick structure. "Get someone to build a hospital, and I'll come and run it."

"We've got the clinic. You can join me there. Doc is getting older. I'm sure he'd love more days to fish." Sage wrapped her arm around her sister. "Don't worry. Something will go your way soon."

"Small town life is not my thing. I have big dreams that can't be found in a place like Aspen Cove." Lydia looked at them. "No offense, but there's nothing here for me."

She was so wrong. Everything worth having was here. Friends, families, and Dalton. Especially Dalton. "That can change. Someone could buy this and turn it into something amazing." She closed her eyes and pictured the building divided into shops, an art gallery, and maybe a culinary school.

While they ran, Samantha listened to Sage and Lydia talk about the shortage of job offers in Denver, and Lydia's frustration with her boyfriend's lack of attention and assistance given he was in charge of the emergency room staffing.

They ran past the park Katie funded. It would be finished before the warm weather hit and provide a safe place for the local children to play. It would offer an opportunity for mothers and fathers to leave their houses and engage with others.

There wasn't much to do in Aspen Cove, so people hibernated inside their homes. Most likely, they weren't eleven seasons behind on *Supernatural. What could they be watching?*

As they neared their homes, they said their goodbyes. They were all excited about karaoke night at the bar. Even Samantha thought it would be fun to sing without expectation. The only one in the group who knew her true identity was Katie, and she hadn't talked.

Samantha's phone buzzed with an incoming message from Deanna because her mother would never text.

Trouble

She wasted no time texting her when a call would be quicker.

"What's up?" Samantha asked as soon as her assistant answered.

Deanna let out a long, breathy exhale. "A few things. Dave is furious that you're not returning his calls, emails, or smoke signals."

Samantha ran up the stairs and entered her cabin. "I'm on vacation, he can wait."

"That's the problem. He's not good at waiting."

She walked back to her room and sat on the edge of the bed. "That's where you come in as my loyal, hard-working assistant with integrity made from steel and resolve made from titanium."

While they talked, Samantha looked through her closet. She didn't miss her stage clothes, but there was a pair of thigh high boots she was certain would knock Dalton flat if he could see them on her. She wished Deanna had packed those.

"That's another problem."

"What? Tell him I'm on vacation, and I'll be at the charity event as planned."

"I can't tell him."

"Why the hell not?" Samantha rarely swore, but anything to do with Dave Belton gave her selective Tourette's.

"He fired me today."

"He can't fire you!" Her voice rose two octaves. "You work for me."

"Yes, but I'm paid by them. So technically, I work for them."

There was no way Samantha could live without her assistant. The woman was a wonder of the world. Without her, Samantha's life would crumble.

"All right, you're hired. Whatever you were making before, give yourself a twenty-five percent raise." Money was the least of Samantha's worries—Dave Belton was her primary problem. If he thought he could bully her into the studio before she had time to relax and regroup, he had another thing coming.

"Thanks, Boss," Deanna said. "There's another problem."

Samantha leaned against the wall and tapped her head gently against the surface. Too hard, and she'd leave a mark and that wouldn't go well with whatever she planned to wear to seduce Dalton tonight.

"I'm ready. Tell me."

"So, apparently you were at a restaurant called Chachi's, which sounded awful until I looked up the menu. I mean, Happy Fries? Those sound amazing."

"They were." She loved Chachi's. It was her second date with Dalton. She pulled a pink, low-cut cashmere sweater from the shelf. She had a friend in high school who reserved a certain sweater for third dates. This little pink number would be hers. With that solved, she returned to the problem at hand.

"Dining at Chachi's was a problem?"

"Only because you walked off stage and disappeared. The tabloids offered up cash for your location. It would be a problem if a waiter named Todd, who has an unhealthy obsession with a once blue-haired singer who happened to snap a selfie with him, threatened to blackmail you if you don't agree to a date with him."

She threw the pink sweater on the bed and rummaged through her jeans to find the perfect pair. Muffins and ice cream and candy along with bacon and pancakes and Happy Fries weren't weight-maintenance foods.

"Are you there?" Deanna asked.

Samantha shook the thoughts of Dalton and Happy Fries from her head. "Yes, and he's ridiculous if he thinks I'm going on a date with him."

"He wrote, and I quote, 'I'm prepared to keep her location secret if she'll meet me for dinner.' Which means he'll sell the picture and your location if you don't."

Samantha knew her time to remain anonymous was coming to an end, but she refused to toss in the towel right now. She also refused to let a pimply-faced teenager blackmail her.

"Tell him no. Chachi's is in a town almost an hour away. He only knows I was there for lunch. I could have been passing through."

"Okay, Boss. What do you want me to tell Dave?"

"Nothing. I'll take care of Dave. You no longer answer to him. Pass on your promotion to the team and let them know to contact you directly if they have questions."

"Will do." There was a breath of silence between them. "Any more of those hot kisses?"

Samantha smiled knowing Deanna couldn't see her bigger-than-life grin, but she knew she'd hear it in her voice. "Those lips have skills, girlfriend. He's so freaking hot."

"I need pictures and details," Deanna squealed.

"I'll see what I can do. Are we good?"

"For now." They hung up.

Samantha sat on the bed and thought about the high-handed tactics Dave used to get her to behave. There was so much abuse in the world.

Abuse of power.

Verbal abuse.

Physical abuse.

Emotional abuse.

She'd seen it all. Experienced much of it. It was time to stop it. Here she thought Marina needed to deal with her problem, and yet Samantha hadn't dealt with her own. Things would be different from now on. Dave Belton could no longer hurt her.

She pulled her old phone from the drawer and powered it up. It sang with the ring of incoming messages for minutes. She ignored them all.

She thought about what she would say, but there was no way to say everything that needed to be said in a text, so she wrote what was in her heart.

Dave,

You have worked me to death for ten years. Add to that the verbal abuse and the total disregard for my general health and welfare, and you can't fault me for wanting to take a break.

If you think firing my assistant will earn my submission, you're wrong. You've fired the first shot in a battle you won't win. Try to sell a concert without a singer.

My commitment to you ends after the charity event and the final album.

Let me rest and find clarity, and maybe we can negotiate a path forward.

Samantha

She powered down her phone with shaking hands. Not once had she had the courage to stand up to him. Even now, she took the coward's way out by texting. If they were face-to-face, she would have seen the vein bulge in his forehead and she would have caved. That's why she needed time and space. Dave Belton kept her close to keep her under control. *Baby steps.*

Walking off that stage and into the crowd was the bravest decision she ever made. But it was also a cowardly move because instead of facing the enemy, she hid from him in a crush of twenty thousand fans. *Baby steps.*

It took five minutes for her racing heart to settle. She calmed her nerves with a glass of wine and went to work getting ready for her date. They hadn't categorized it as an actual date, but he texted her and reminded her that he'd be there at six. That sounded like a date.

She squeezed into a pair of skinny jeans, pulled on the softest sweater she'd ever bought, and slipped on the same ankle boots she'd worn at her last concert. Though the boots looked fine, she still wished she had the calfskin, leather thigh-highs.

Hair down, watermelon gloss applied, she waited by the door for Dalton. Something told her tonight would be one to remember.

Who would have believed that Indigo was nervous? Then again, Indigo wasn't here. Samantha was, and she had a taste of perfection when she slept in Dalton's strong arms. Arms that did nothing but hold her tight and cradle her while she slept. He asked nothing of her. He didn't take advantage of her. He laid beside her and made her feel like she mattered.

At exactly six o'clock, he knocked. She counted to ten, not wanting to seem too eager. When she opened the door, he stood in front of her wearing jeans that made her body tingle. The denim hugged all the places she wanted to touch.

In his hand was a bouquet filled with yellow roses, irises, and baby's breath—a beautiful combination of flowers. He pressed them forward.

"They're beautiful. Thank you." He followed her to the kitchen, where she filled the biggest glass she had with water and arranged the flowers before she set them on the table.

"They reminded me of you."

"These reminded you of me?"

"Yes, the irises are so dark blue, they're almost black, like your eyes. The yellow roses are like the sun, warm and happy—like your personality. The baby's breath flowers are tiny, with a touch of innocence, but so beautiful. And ..." He rubbed his hands over them, and they sprung back into place. "They're resilient too." He thumbed her chin so she looked up at him. He brushed a tender kiss over her lips. "Shall we go?"

She picked up her purse from the table. "Yes. I'm ready to hear you sing."

"Not happening, sweetheart."

She exaggerated a pout. "And I thought you would serenade me."

"Later I'll make your body sing, but me sing? Not on your life. Let's go before I change my mind and lock us inside." He stepped back and took her in. "You look so damn hot, I don't think I want to share you with anyone."

"We could stay here ..."

"It's karaoke night. No one misses it unless the owner is ice fishing, which he's not, so it's a go. If we don't show up, someone will send out a search party, or the sheriff will come since he's such a fan. This town takes its showmanship seriously."

"We should go before Sheriff Cooper comes again with lights flashing."

Dalton helped her into her jacket and walked her to his truck. Once inside, he leaned in and kissed her dizzy. "Just a taste of what's coming."

"Are you sure we have to go?"

"We do, but we'll leave as soon as we can. You can claim to have a stomachache. Sage is bringing dinner."

She reached across the space and gave him a soft punch to the arm. "That's an awful thing to say."

He pulled out of the driveway and headed downtown. "Tell me that after you've eaten her lasagna."

"It can't be that bad."

He chuckled. "You'll see."

In minutes, they were there. Samantha was shocked to see how many people lived in town. The bar was full. Cannon, Bowie, and Sage stood behind the bar, pulling pitchers of beer and filling shot glasses.

The man she knew as "Doc" was on the stage singing "Hound Dog" rather poorly. They made their way to the bar, where a glass of wine and a beer sat waiting.

Sage took Samantha's purse and served her a plate of lasagna. "I brought dinner."

Samantha looked at the tinfoil baking tray on the back counter, then glanced at Dalton. He gave her an I-told-you-so look. She forked a bite from her plate and put it into her mouth. Not only was it horrid, but it was still frozen in the center. "So good." She faked a smile and washed it down with a sip of wine, then passed the plate to Dalton. "I ate already, but Dalton said he was famished."

He pulled her barstool next to him. "You're going to pay for that." He took a bite and smiled. When Sage turned around, he fed the food to Otis, who sat begging at his feet. The dog wasn't picky.

When Doc finished his song, he called the next victim. It was a quirky Aspen Cove tradition to choose the song and the next singer. After much help from the girls, Doc chose Bowie as the next one up in the round robin. Then Katie took the stage to sing an old Freda Payne song called "Band of Gold."

Samantha knew she was in trouble when Katie pointed to her and smiled. She knew she wouldn't get away without singing. The question was, would she get away unrecognized?

Dalton reached for her. "Don't go. It's a trap. She'll give you some impossible song to sing just to break you in."

"I've got this." She gave him a passing kiss and went to the small stage to take the mic. When the Whitney Houston song "Queen of the Night" played, she groaned. Katie would pay for this somehow.

There were two ways to attack this song. Belt it out like the pro she was, or croak it out like everyone expected. She'd given nothing less than her best performance, so why stop now?

The words flowed from her so raw—so true. As she sang, everyone in the bar faded until only Dalton remained. His eyes connected with hers. The lyrics poured out of her like they were written for him. He had the stuff that she wanted—the stuff that she needed. She knew it was too early to feel such strong emotions, but he was the first man to see her as a person.

She couldn't keep him—that was a certainty. Her life was so far removed from his. All she had was now. She would leave nothing behind and carry no regrets forward.

When she hit the chorus, the crowd cheered. Dollar bills floated through the air. She'd never been paid so little for a performance she enjoyed so much. The music had become a burden, but tonight it freed her.

When the song finished, she tossed the mic to Sheriff Cooper and walked over to Dalton. "I'm ready to leave."

Dalton nearly fell off his chair. He pulled a twenty from his pocket and set it on the counter. Sage passed him Samantha's purse, and all eyes watched them as they worked their way through the crowd. This time, she wasn't running *away* but running *to*—the best night of her life.

CHAPTER FIFTEEN

Her beautiful voice continued to replay in his head all the way home. Her eyes pierced his soul as if she sang the words to him. A song about what she wanted and needed.

"Wow." He reached over and held her hand. "That was ... that was amazing. You have quite a voice."

"Thank you."

He couldn't believe that voice inside her tiny body could be so big. "You should be a singer."

She giggled. "I sing. I am a singer. I sang to you."

Knowing that song was for him filled him with warmth. Though she didn't choose it, she sang it like she meant every word. He got all choked up when she looked at him like he was special. It felt so real that a lump the size of Wyoming lodged in his throat.

It was too soon to think about love, but he knew if there was ever a chance of falling in love with anyone, it would be easy to fall in love with Samantha. Hell, he was halfway there already. Bowie and Cannon were right. Dalton was whipped, and he hadn't even been inside her yet.

He pulled up in front of his cabin and killed the engine. "I thought we could stay at my place tonight." He held his breath. It was a forgone conclusion that they'd be together tonight. He wanted it. He thought she wanted it.

"Are you inviting me for a sleepover, Dalton?" She looked at him beneath long onyx lashes.

He wasn't the blushing type, but he swore there was heat on his cheeks. "I'll make you breakfast in the morning."

Everything about Samantha was near perfect. She was by far too skinny, but he could solve that with home-cooked meals. Most perfect was her ability to take him out at the knees with a smile.

"Pancakes?"

"Are you negotiating?"

"I'd be silly not to."

"Anything. You can have anything." He jumped out of his truck and rushed around to her side to open her door.

"I need a few things from my place."

He stood in front of her while she slid from the truck into his body. They walked hand-in-hand to her door. On the porch was a single daisy. She bent over to pick it up. "Must have fallen from my bouquet." She twirled it around and brought it to her nose.

Dalton knew for a fact the flower didn't come from her bouquet. He looked around and wondered whose ass he'd have to kick.

Once inside, she pressed the flower into the glass with the others and walked back to her room. The only thing she came out with was a toothbrush.

"Low-maintenance. My kind of girl." In the silence of the cabin he heard her stomach growl. She'd only had a bite of poison lasagna. "And you're hungry. I can fix that too."

"Are you going to solve all my problems tonight?"

"I'm going to try." He squatted down and wrapped his arms around her bottom before he stood. She lifted her hand so she wouldn't hit the ceiling, but she knew he'd let nothing happen to her. When he loosened his hold, she slid down his body until they were face to face. One quick kiss in the middle of her entryway would not satisfy the hunger he had for her. A kiss wouldn't fill her belly, but it was a kiss that spoke of their need for each other. When she ran her hands through his hair and pulled him deeper into the kiss, he knew he had to get her out of here or they'd never leave her cabin.

He loosened his hold until her boots hit the scarred wooden floor. "Ready?"

She licked her lips like she was savoring the taste of him. "So ready. You have no idea."

Every time she was near him, he got hard. That alone gave him plenty of ideas. Before he changed his mind and stayed, he led her to the doorway. He glanced back at the flowers on the table. *Could there have been a daisy in the mix?*

He held his breath when he opened the door to his world. He'd never had a woman in his house or his bed. This was his safe haven. A place where the outside world wasn't invited in. And yet ... here he was opening it up to her.

She walked past him into the entryway. He closed the door behind them. He'd never felt so right about something or someone.

"Wow. This place is amazing."

He looked at his home through her eyes. It was pretty amazing. More so because while he sat in prison, the work on his house continued. His mom oversaw the laborers as they turned his run-down shack into a home. *"That's what moms do,"* she told him when he tried to argue with her about the time and expense.

They were partners at Maisey's, and during the tourist season they made a killing. The building was paid off. Other than utilities and taxes, the place was pure profit. He wasn't rich by any means, but he didn't need much to keep him happy.

"You like it?"

She held up her toothbrush. "I should have packed all my stuff and moved over here. Your house is a five-star hotel. Mine is more like a bunk house at summer camp."

"You went to camp?"

Her head shook. "No, we couldn't afford it, but I looked at

brochures. Dreaming costs nothing." That statement reminded her of Marina.

"Our lives weren't much different. Abusive fathers and determined mothers. No camp for me either."

She nodded. "And we survived." She thumbed the scar above his eye.

"Yes, we did." He lowered her hand and wrapped it in his. "Want the tour?"

"Absolutely."

They walked across his shiny oak floors into the living room, where his leather couch took up most of the space. A wall of glass looked over the lake. He lowered the blinds to give them privacy. He had a big screen television on his wall hanging above the fireplace.

"Yours is so big." She teased him, and he loved it.

"Size matters."

"I've heard that."

He squeezed her hand and led her into the galley kitchen. Only his was filled with top-of-the-line appliances.

"You have a microwave." She never thought she'd ever get excited over something as simple as an appliance, but the stainless steel box sitting over his stove made her giddy.

"I've got it all." He stood tall as he bantered with her.

"We'll see." She brushed past him, running her fingers over the granite counter.

"I'll show you after I feed you." He placed his hands on her hips and lifted her onto the countertop next to the stove. "Sit here. Watch and be amazed."

"Is the tour finished already? I thought maybe ..." She bit her lip. "Maybe I'd see your bedroom."

"Sweetheart, if we got to the bedroom, we'd never leave it. Let me be chivalrous and feed you so I can keep you in bed until I have to go to work on Tuesday."

"You're making promises you better be able to keep."

He drew an imaginary X across his chest. "Cross my heart. I'm a man of my word."

She squirmed on the counter while he pulled the ingredients for chicken piccata from the refrigerator. After he put a pot of water to boil on the stovetop, he went about mixing the ingredients for the sauce.

He slid past her and pounded the chicken breasts thin.

"You're killing that chicken."

He hit it a few more times. "That's what I do. I kill things." He was referring to food, but the irony wasn't lost on him.

Each time he had to pass her, he stopped for a kiss. Each kiss became more than the one before it. She tasted like fine wine. It could be because he had poured her a glass while he cooked or maybe because she was a fine vintage all on her own.

"How is it that you're not with someone?" He drained the pasta he'd cooked and plated up their dinner.

"I'm far too busy. My job takes me around the world, but I'm making some changes. It would be so nice to make a living *and* have a life."

After the final sprinkle of fresh herbs, he lowered her to her feet and walked her over to his small dining table by the window that overlooked the lake like hers. Everything beautiful about the cabins could be found in their back halves, on the lakeside. The front door led to nothing more exciting than a hallway.

He pulled out her chair and served her dinner. Watching her eat was an orgasmic experience. She hummed and moaned, and each bite made him harder.

"I take it you like it?"

"Oh my God, can I keep you? You want to go on tour with me?" She swallowed a sip of wine. "I mean go on my business trips. You can be my personal chef."

"Does the job pay in kisses?"

"Are you negotiating?"

Dalton chuckled. "I'd be silly not to."

"Then I'd ask for more than kisses."

He poured her another glass of wine and cleared her empty plate.

"I'll interview you tonight before I decide what goes on my list of demands. A comprehensive benefit package can make a difference."

She offered him her hand. "Shall we begin?"

CHAPTER SIXTEEN

Thump.

Thump.

Thump.

Samantha's heart beat like a tribal drum. She wasn't normally so forward and brazen, but her time was running out, and she wanted what she wanted. That was Dalton for as long as she could keep him.

Something about sending that text to Dave Benton freed her. Like ten years worth of chains simply broke loose. She deserved to be happy. Dalton made her happy.

He was selfless and kind and sexy. He kissed like a master. When his hands roamed her body, it was as if he'd wanted to memorize every part of her.

"Stay here for a second." He left her standing by the window, looking out over the lake. Small fires dotted the ice where diehard fishermen grabbed on to the last chance to pull a trophy from beneath the frozen surface.

Dalton returned in minutes and walked her down the hallway. Shadows of light danced across the walls of the room. He'd lit candles. Her heart burst with happiness. When had anything been so perfect?

"Do you do this for all your women?"

He cupped her cheek and looked into her eyes. His hard blue eyes softened. "No, you are the first woman in my house. The first I've invited to my bed. The first to break through my icy heart."

She couldn't breathe. His words had twisted inside her, tightening a hold on her heart. "I've never been treated like this. You're going to spoil me."

"I plan to."

He walked her to his bed until the mocha brown comforter hit the back of her knees. She leaned back and let his soft mattress hug her body. Her hands flattened onto the fabric. This is where she wanted to be, and she hoped he kept his promise of keeping her here all weekend.

Propped on her elbows, she watched him remove his shirt. The soft light created shadows that only increased her awareness of how toned and fit he was. The candlelight danced over the ridges and valleys of his carved-from-rock body.

"You work out?" She felt stupid for asking. With a body like his, he had to spend hours in the gym.

"I used to. I don't so much now. There was a time where all I did was work out."

"You're beautiful." She wanted to take the words back. What man wanted to be called beautiful?

"No, you're beautiful." He lifted her feet one at a time and tossed her boots aside. "Even when you had blue hair, I thought you were beautiful."

"You like it better blue?" She watched him unbuckle his belt and pull it through the loops. He rolled it up and walked it over to his dresser. Dalton wasn't what she expected. His house wasn't what she expected. He was put-together. His house was clean—almost military or institutional in its organization—but there was a warmth to everything he did. He invested himself.

"No, I like this better, but I still thought you were beautiful."

She rolled to her side to stare at him. "Was that before or after you called me a skinny, blue-haired boy?"

He stalked toward her. She rolled onto her back in time for him to straddle her hips. With one motion he pulled her pink, cashmere, third-date sweater over her head and cupped the pink lacy bra she wore.

"These," he said with a heat and gravel voice, "would never belong to a boy."

"No? Just the hair, huh?"

He rubbed his thumbs over her aroused peaks. "Was that a phase?"

A ten-year phase. "I was definitely going through something. I'm working through it." She was making headway through her life. It wouldn't be easy, but she knew it would be worth it. Maybe she could figure out a way to keep Dalton.

"I'll work you through it." He reached behind her to unhook her bra. "As pretty as that little piece of lace is, I find you even more beautiful naked." He made fast work of removing her clothes.

"We are not doing this again." She rose up and tugged at the button of his jeans, then pulled the zipper down. "You may have the patience of a saint, but I don't. It's been a very long time for me, and you've been stroking my libido since the start."

He rolled off the bed and pulled down his pants until all he wore was a pair of clingy boxers. Her eyes went straight for the goods.

Oh shit. She knew he was well-endowed, but she never imagined that what she saw outlined down his thigh would be so big.

He opened the drawer to his nightstand and pulled out a strip of condoms. Magnum size, of course. "I stocked up."

"Oh shit."

He tugged his boxers off, evening the playing field. They were both naked. And she was scared to death.

"Changing your mind?" His lips twitched in amusement.

She pulled a deep breath into her lungs and thought of the words he'd told her days ago. "No. A really sexy man told me I could always make room for what I desired. And I want you. All of you."

"That's my girl." He climbed onto the bed beside her.

She knew Dalton wasn't a dive-straight-in kind of guy. He'd told her more than once that he loved the in-between. As he left kisses across her body, she grew fond of it as well. She'd never had the time to lie in bed and be worshipped by a man. Never had she wanted a man to kiss her as much as she wanted Dalton.

"This thing between us is dangerous," he said against her neck. "You're fire, and I'm accelerant."

Not wanting to be a taker and not a giver, she switched places with him. As she straddled his waist, his length sat heavy and ready between her legs. It would have been so easy to lift up and let it all happen, but she wanted Dalton to feel as cherished as she did.

Her fingers ghosted over his skin until goose bumps rose beneath her touch. She traced his tattoos. He was a work of art. "Did these hurt?"

He opened his heavy lids to look at her. "Not like you'd think. It's a good kind of pain."

Leaning forward, she pressed her breasts to his chest. The fine dusting of dark hair grazed her sensitive peaks. "If you gave me a tattoo, what would it be?" She drew her tongue over his nipple, and he hissed.

"Can't think." His hands reached for her bottom and squeezed. He pulled her harder against his length and groaned.

His expression was a mixture of pain and pleasure. "Don't think." She shimmied down his body and kissed him where he needed attention the most. "Just feel."

"You're killing me."

She ran her tongue down the length of him. "Maybe, but you'll die happy," she purred against his silky soft skin.

Before she could take him inside her mouth, she was flat on her back and Dalton was over her. He reached for a foil wrapper and tore the end off with his teeth.

His breath sucked in when she helped him roll it on. Settled between her thighs, she opened to invite him in, more than ready for this moment.

At first, she was certain he'd split her in half, but he took his time coaxing her body to relax around him. He eased into her slowly. He was right, there was always room for what she desired.

Never in her life had she felt so complete. They moved together the way a melody and lyrics complemented each other.

"So good," she whispered against his chest. She rose to meet his thrusts.

She gripped his hips and pulled him in as close and deep as she could get him. She wanted him to live inside her. He was right, this was dangerous because now that she knew how it could be with two people who shared a connection, she wanted more. Did she dare to dream for more?

His steady rhythm pushed her passion forward. He never took his eyes off her. That alone pushed her to the edge. Possessive and feral was how he looked as he claimed her. For that moment in time she belonged to him. She was his. She wanted to be his forever.

Writhing and panting beneath him caused a sheen of sweat on her brow. His glorious body pumped into her with a purpose. Shocks of pleasure stole what breaths remained in her lungs. He pushed her to the limits, pulled her to the edge, and eased her back countless times. He didn't hurry. It was as if her pleasure was more important to him than anything in the world.

So close to falling off the edge. So close to falling in love. She held her breath for a moment, hoping to capture every feeling racing through her. As her body took control and her muscles ceased and then shook, she exploded around him. Her vision blurred, then blackened until prisms of light danced behind her eyelids. She knew she'd seen heaven.

She held tight until Dalton's hard body heaved forward and stilled. Most men have an expression when they climax. Often, it's not attractive. She swore she'd never seen a smile so beautiful as the one Dalton gave her when he found his release.

He didn't collapse on top of her but gently pulled out and lay down beside her. She curled into his arms, where she was content to stay forever.

His fingers brushed over her skin until he came to the place above her heart. He lingered there. She leaned back and looked into his eyes —eyes that told more than he did. Their experience went far deeper than good sex. It spoke of their deep connection. She saw it in his face. Felt it in her heart.

"Your tattoo would say, 'Dalton's.'" He pressed his hand over her heart. "Right here."

Never had she been so moved. People wanted her talent. They wanted her money. No one had ever asked for her heart. "After what you did, my heart belongs to you." She didn't mean to say it out loud. She spoke without thought, without fear—something she rarely did because she'd learned from watching her mother that speaking the truth was often painful. "You've ruined me, Dalton Black."

He brushed the damp hair back from her forehead. "Likewise, Samantha White."

"You're black, I'm white, but it's the gray in-between where the magic happens."

He nuzzled her neck. "I'm a fan of the gray."

Over the next several days, he showed her how lovely the color gray could be. When Sage and Katie and Lydia stopped by, he told them she was his until Tuesday. Little did he know, he'd claimed her for life.

CHAPTER SEVENTEEN

Dalton knew he had to share Samantha when Sage and Lydia banged on the door early Tuesday morning requiring proof of life. Lydia was heading back to Denver to continue her job search and wanted to say goodbye. She'd been tight-lipped about her prospects, which made him think they weren't good.

It was Tuesday, which meant Dalton was cooking at the diner. As he flipped pancakes, he thought about the tiny little firecracker he'd loved on all weekend. Pulled in two different directions, he was in a quandary about telling Samantha about his past. They agreed to keep their secrets, but it weighed heavily on his mind. What she thought of him was important. Would the truth bother her? He didn't want to spoil what they had. They connected on a deep level. After a week, they were finishing each other's sentences. He'd never had that with anyone. Not even Casey, the woman he'd dated for two years.

Maisey walked through the swinging doors. "Your girlfriend is here with the gang."

He liked the sound of Samantha being called his girlfriend. It was the furthest thing from the truth, but it warmed him through and through to consider the possibility.

"I wish." He put Doc's pancakes on the counter and brushed his hands on his apron. Making sure nothing would start on fire while he was gone, he left the kitchen behind him to get a kiss from his 'girlfriend'.

She never ceased to take his breath away. Today, she was dressed in jeans and a black T-shirt that hung off one shoulder. On closer inspection, he realized it was his T-shirt, and that did something to him. Seeing her in his clothes made him want to stick out his chest and pound it.

He lengthened his stride to get to her faster. At the table, he ignored Sage and Katie and gave Samantha a kiss.

"I'd say get a room, but then we might not see you two for months." Katie poked Dalton in the arm. Since she and Sage were on the same side of the booth, he slid in next to Samantha.

"You hungry, sweetheart?" She nodded. Lord knows she must be because they had burned enough calories.

Sage waved her hand in front of his face. "We're here too."

"I see ya." He didn't really, but he knew they were there. "What do you want?"

Katie let out a growl of frustration. "No sweetheart for us?"

He looked at Katie. "Bowie's across the street for you." His eyes went to Sage. "No idea where you've hidden Cannon."

"How have you missed him? He's like you, big as a tank. Not likely I can hide him anywhere. Today, he's in our garage whittling."

Katie jumped up and down in her seat. "I get all the ornaments. I'll pay double." She'd bought every ornament he'd put on consignment. By the time Christmas rolled around, she had the tree covered in whittled wood wildlife and angels.

Dalton turned to Samantha. "How about a waffle and bacon?" He cupped her face and ran his thumb across her cheek. "Or I can make that omelet you love."

"Waffle, please."

"Anything you want, baby." He slid out of the booth but not

before claiming another kiss. He turned to Sage and Katie. "Have you decided?"

"Waffles and bacon all the way around." He was several steps away when he heard Katie declare, "That boy has it bad for you."

He couldn't argue an obvious truth. He was falling in love with Samantha White. He loved the feeling yet hated the situation because what they had could never be long-term. He had commitments and responsibilities in Aspen Cove, not to mention four more years of parole check-ins. She had a life outside the little cocoon she'd created here. A life without him.

With the waffles done and the bacon crisp, he placed a strawberry on the top of each except for Samantha's. On hers, he made a smiley face out of several berries because that's how he felt with her around. He had finally found happiness.

With a few more orders to fill, he flicked at the bell to alert his mom to an order up. When he was free again, he peeked out the swinging doors to find the table vacant and a feeling of emptiness echoed in his heart.

In his favorite booth in the corner sat Doc, reading his paper.

"You gonna stare at me or come and chat?" No one ever got anything past Doc. He was old, not blind, and he had a spooky sixth sense about these things. He knew more than Abby Garrett—and she knew everything.

"What's up?" Adding "Doc" to the end of the sentence seemed cliché, so he let it end there.

"The population of Aspen Cove is up." He chuckled. "Soon, we'll be back to where we were twenty years ago." He sat back and placed his hands on his belly. "Those were the days."

"For some of you. Not so good for Mom and me." Twenty years ago, his dad was still alive.

"It's a good thing your old man died immediately because I'm not sure I would have tried to save the bastard."

Dalton's eyes grew large. He'd never heard Doc talk negatively about anyone. "Yes, you would have. That's what you do."

Doc pruned his lips and nodded. "You're probably right, but I would have made sure his recovery was long and painful."

"I never understood how some people could be so evil."

"Like the man you hit?"

Dalton's shoulders sagged. "You mean the man I killed."

Doc's eyebrows lifted. They always seemed ready to take flight. "Now, son, I don't see it that way."

Dalton knew from experience that if Doc started with "Now, son", he was in teaching mode. It was a good thing the diner had slowed down because Doc's lessons rarely finished fast.

"It is what it is."

Doc shook his head. "Things are seldom what they seem. That man killed himself. There are lowlifes, and—no offense to your mom—I'd have categorized Ben in that group when he was drinking. Not so much now. Andy Kranz was worse. He was a *no* life. That man was rancid hamburger meat. You did the world a favor by tossing out the trash. It's a shame you had to do time, but I'm not sure it was a bad thing, either."

"You think the time I did served me well?"

"I think it could have gone several ways. I think you spent a lot of time deciding the type of man you wanted to be. You got a degree in business management, which can't hurt running Maisey's. You grew up."

"I also have a felony conviction and no real earning potential."

"Should I get you a Kleenex? I've never known you to whine. Why now?"

The statement made him bristle because never once did Dalton take the time to have a pity party.

"You're right. The problem is, I've never had to worry about it. Now that Samantha is in my life … it changes things."

"She's a keeper. She's tough like you and knows life's not fair. Does she have a problem with your record?" Doc looked at the empty booth where she'd once sat. "She didn't look like she had a problem when you two were canoodling."

"I haven't told her. Do you think I should?"

"Can't say. Only you know the answer to that question, but I'm sure it would be easier hearing the truth from the person who lived it."

Doc pushed his legs to the edge of the bench and started a rocking motion that propelled him up and forward. His age was showing.

"Damn body won't work like it used to."

Dalton picked up the dirty dishes and walked behind Doc. "Good thing your mind's sharp as a tack."

"If my mind ever falters, kill me." His eyes popped when he realized what he'd said.

"You'll have to find someone else. I'm out of that business."

Doc walked out. Dalton went back to the kitchen.

His mom leaned against the prep table eating a piece of apple pie.

"Samantha says she'll be at the bakery when you get off."

He looked at the clock and frowned. He still had two hours left on his shift. His disappointment must have been obvious. "Thanks, Mom." He walked behind the burners to start his breakfast cleanup, but it was already done. "You cleaned my station?"

Maisey ignored his question. "You like her, don't you?"

"More than I should."

"I like her too. Go get her and have fun. Life's way too short. I got this."

Dalton was already untying his apron. "Are you sure?"

"The only one coming in is Abby, and she'll want coffee and pie. Ben will be here, but he can help himself. He's getting handy in the kitchen."

"You replacing me?"

She walked up to him and kissed him on the cheek. "Not possible. Now go get your girl."

He didn't have to be told twice. He tossed his apron on the prep table and bolted for the front door.

He found Samantha sitting under the Wishing Wall, filling out notes. So immersed in her task, he went unnoticed until he kissed her cheek.

She looked up, startled. "You're early."

He sat in the chair across from her. "I couldn't wait."

"I'm glad."

She had dozens of folded notes in front of her. Dalton wondered if they were her wishes.

"Can I grant any of those?"

Her lush lips broadened into a bright smile. She rummaged through the pile and pulled out one and handed it to him.

Across the center of the pink paper it read:

I wish for endless kisses from Dalton Black.

"Granted. You want to start those here and go back home?" It was funny how his place had become their home in days. It felt right.

She passed another note to him.

I wish Dalton would take me for a ride on his motorcycle.

"You're easy."

"Yes, but I'm not cheap."

He looked over his shoulder. The day was perfect for a ride. "Let's go. I'll give you the ride of a lifetime."

She gathered her notes and stuffed them inside her bag.

"I think you've given me one already. I'm interested in a simple trip around the lake with my body pressed to yours. Katie tells me there's nothing like the wind in my hair and a Harley between my legs."

"I used to think that was nirvana. That was before I met you and settled between your legs."

"You're such a flirt." She walked to the door and opened and closed it several times. The bell rang a few times before Katie walked in from the storage room.

She came forward, patting Sahara on the back. "You leaving?"

Dalton's heart stopped when she wrapped her arms around him and said, "My man's taking me for a ride."

Her man. If there were ever a chest-pounding moment, it was that second she claimed him.

"I like being your man."

When they got to his cabin, he didn't go inside because he knew once they were behind closed doors, the first kiss would lead to more, and they'd never leave. Samantha's wish was to ride on the back of his Harley. That was easy to grant. When they got back, he'd work on the endless kisses.

CHAPTER EIGHTEEN

Never in her existence had she been so free. On the back of Dalton's Harley, she held on for dear life, let the wind blow in her hair, and lived honestly—well, mostly honestly.

They stopped at points along the way where Dalton pointed out landmarks like the cove surrounded by aspens for which the town was named.

On the far side of the lake, he pulled into a parking lot where a single wooden shack sat surrounded by picnic tables and trash cans. An old tin sign that read, 'Sam's Scoops' hung over the open window. Leaning across the counter was a middle-aged man who hadn't seen a razor or scissors in years.

"Dalton, my man." He nearly fell out of the shack trying to fist bump Dalton.

"Sam, what's the flavor of the day?"

"I'd say it's her." He nodded toward Samantha. "She looks good."

"She's mine." Dalton wrapped his arms possessively around Samantha.

"Well, then." He turned around and pointed to the sign, "if you're talking ice cream, I've got Breakfast in Bed, which is maple ice cream with donut pieces and glazed bacon; Lickin' Lizard, which is vanilla ice cream and gummy worms; and Unicorn Poop, which is basically rocky road with the addition of Pop Rocks." He smiled at them like he'd recited a Pulitzer Prize–winning novel. "What's your poison?"

The horror on her face must have been obvious. Who in their right mind wanted to eat anything called Unicorn Poop, or worms—gummy or not? The breakfast flavor didn't sound half bad if the ingredients were served individually.

"Trust me?" Dalton winked at her.

Her trust wasn't given lightly, but she did trust him with everything. "I do."

"We'll take a scoop of each." He looked at Samantha. "You haven't lived until you've tasted Sam's ice cream."

"My fear is I won't live *after* I've tasted it."

"I heard that, young lady." Sam's gravelly voice gave her the impression he hadn't missed a smoke in years. He pushed a plastic bowl forward and sprinkled something chocolate coated on top. "A little something extra." He smiled wide enough for his overgrown beard to split and show his lips and teeth. "Chocolate covered ants. You'll love the texture."

Dalton paid, picked up the bowl and led her to a table where they sat side by side.

Her lip curled in disgust. "I'm not eating bugs."

"No ants, only chocolate covered crispy rice." Dalton scooped a spoon of Unicorn Poop and pressed it to her mouth. "Open up."

Her tongue darted out to grab the tiniest taste. When the chocolate hit and the Pop Rocks burst, she was sold. "That's amazing."

They shared bite after bite until the bowl was empty.

"Did I lie?"

"I'm not sure you have it in you to lie."

His expression turned serious. "Not about ice cream."

There was something behind his statement—something that he was keeping to himself. She couldn't fault him. She hadn't divulged everything about herself either. Rather than dwell on the past, she dug right into her critique. "I love Unicorn Poop." She made a face. "Can't believe I said that." She dipped her finger into the bowl to swipe up an 'ant'. Before she could put it into her mouth, Dalton wrapped his lips around her finger and sucked it clean. Every cell in her body lit on fire. His tongue had the kind of talent that should be boxed and sold. "Breakfast in Bed was good, but I prefer yours. Not a huge fan of the worms, only because they're hard to chew when they're cold."

He looked at her with lazy bedroom eyes. It was the same look that melted her into the bed each night.

"And I thought you were a fan of hard worms."

"Really?" She knuckled him in the chest. Not hard enough to hurt but enough for him to feel it. "You're not giving yourself enough credit."

"Are you defending my manhood?" The aw-shucks look didn't fit the big man at her side.

"Just telling it like it is. Now take me home and show off your worm."

Dalton moved quickly when motivated, and anything to do with her and him naked had him focused.

The forty-five minutes it took to get there seemed like only twenty to get home. He pulled into her driveway so she could run inside and get some clean clothes. When she got to the door, Samantha stopped cold. It was cracked open, and her latest album played in the background.

She scurried backward.

Dalton watched her return. "Looking for one of those endless kisses?"

Her heart pounded in her chest. Blood pumped so hard, she heard nothing but the *whoosh* in her ears. Words caught in her throat.

"What's wrong?" He looked past her to the opened door, and he was gone.

She pulled her phone from her bag and dialed the sheriff. She croaked out that someone was in her cabin and Dalton was confronting the intruder.

Sheriff Cooper let out a string of expletives that could make a hooker blush before he said he was on his way.

Samantha was torn between staying put and offering Dalton help. Her mind raced as she played out every scenario. What if it was her manager? What if it was a robber? What if Dalton was in danger? That was the thought that moved her forward and up the steps.

"Get out!" She heard an unrecognizable voice scream. The voice was too high to be Dalton and too low to be female.

She snuck inside the doorway with her phone in her hand. It was ridiculous that her only weapon was a palm-sized plastic box. She shouldn't have worried. Dalton was there, and if he could, he would protect her.

In the corner by the lit fireplace, he towered over a cowering young man. When the intruder saw her, he hopped to his feet and yelled, "Indigo! You're here."

"Todd?" She recognized the kid from Chachi's. "What are you doing here?" Samantha knew what he was doing. He was demanding his date. As she looked around the room, she would have been touched if she weren't so freaked out. A bottle of cheap wine and two glasses sat on the coffee table. A bouquet of daisies replaced the flowers Dalton had given her. That brought a level of anger she didn't know she was capable of, but the worst thing was the framed pictures he'd set around the room. He'd photoshopped a life for them. He'd taken publicity shots and put himself in each one.

Before Todd could answer, Sheriff Cooper burst inside the cabin with his hand on his weapon. He noticed the young man cowering in the corner. "Thank God." He walked to Dalton, who seemed to grow larger by the second and shoved him back. "Go home, Dalton. You don't need this trouble."

"No." The word came out in an angry growl. "I'm not leaving Samantha."

Todd shook his head. "She's not Samantha. That's Indigo." He looked at the sheriff. "I can show you." He pointed to his back pocket.

The sheriff nodded, and Samantha knew everything good about her life would end in seconds. The kid pulled out his wallet and let a strip of photos fall like dominoes. It was an act more suitable for a proud parent than a fan. But Todd wasn't any admirer; he'd proved himself to be a true fanatic.

Dalton lunged forward to grab the photos.

Samantha saw the recognition in his eyes. "It's you."

What could she say but the truth? "Yes, it's me, and I can explain."

He stepped back and looked at her, then did something unexpected. He smiled. "I like the brown hair better."

"Dude, that's Indigo." Todd moved forward, but the sheriff stopped his progress. "Have you heard her sing?"

Dalton's smile widened. "Yes, I have, and it's almost a religious experience." He wrapped his arms around her and whispered, "You could have trusted me with the truth."

"I wanted you to like me for me, not for who everyone thinks I am."

"I more than like you Samantha. I lo—"

"What do you want to do about this one?" Sheriff Cooper interrupted. His hand circled Todd's arm. He dragged him forward. "There is a list of charges you could file, including breaking and entering."

"She can't press charges. I'm a fan."

Samantha stepped forward. Dalton stepped in front of her protectively. Before her eyes, he morphed into a mass of agitation. The tension rolled off him in heated waves.

"I could have killed you." Dalton exchanged looks with the sheriff. "You don't walk into someone's house uninvited. What the hell were you thinking?"

"It's okay." Samantha slid in front of Dalton and placed her hand on his chest. Immediately, his tension eased. "I remember another man rushing into my house uninvited." She turned to Todd. "How old are you?"

"Twenty," he said proudly.

Sheriff Cooper pointed to the alcohol. "Who sold you that?"

"I stole it," Todd said, and then blanched. "I mean, I found it."

"Right." The sheriff turned to Samantha. "You pressing charges?"

Part of her wanted to press charges so Todd would learn a lesson. Part of her figured everyone needed a second chance. "No, but I better not see him again unless he's in the front row of a concert." She tried to give him a wicked mean scowl but couldn't pull it off.

"Let's go." Sheriff Cooper led Todd to the door. The young man reached for a picture he set on the entry table. "Can you sign this?"

"Out," Dalton bellowed.

Todd didn't stall. He rushed out of the house with the sheriff giving him a list of laws he'd broken.

When Samantha turned around, Dalton was scrolling furiously through his phone.

"What are you doing?"

He flopped his big body onto the couch. "I just found out my girlfriend is famous. I'm downloading all your music."

She laughed. "You're crazy."

He pulled her into his lap. "For you."

"Perfect answer." She crawled out of his lap and collected the photos of her fake wedding, her fake Valentine's Day, her fake Christmas, and tossed them into the trash can. The same trash can where Todd had thrown Dalton's flowers. After she exchanged the daisies for the discarded bouquet, she climbed back into Dalton's lap.

"You're not mad?"

"Mad for you." He flipped her around to straddle him like she weighed nothing because in truth, she didn't weigh much. Although, she was certain she had put on a few pounds. How could she not with Dalton constantly feeding her?

"I should have told you the truth."

"You hinted at it in so many ways. If I were a smarter man, I would have listened and understood."

"You pay attention to the important things." She snuggled close to his chest, grateful that her lack of transparency hadn't ruined what they had together.

"How about I take you to bed and you sing me a love song?"

"How about you take me to bed and make my body sing?"

"That'll work." He rose with her in his arms and carried her to her bedroom, where Dalton wasted no time making her body sing.

Exhausted after a night of passion, she fell asleep in the arms of the only man she felt safe around. The only man she trusted. The only man able to unlock her heart.

When a knock on the door woke them both the next morning, Dalton pulled on his T-shirt and his pants and grumbled all the way to the door. "This better be important, or you're dead."

She thought nothing of it until she recognized the click of cameras and the shouts of pushy reporters. This was all Todd's doing. Now she wished she had pressed charges. At least she would have had an additional day or so before the shit hit the fan.

She rushed out the door to rescue Dalton.

"Indigo! How do you think your fans will respond to your relationship with Dalton Black, a convicted killer?"

She staggered back. She was hit with a question that completely floored her, and she had no answer.

"Assholes!" Dalton yelled at the dozen or so reporters camped in front of her house snapping photos. He pulled Samantha into his arms and took her inside where it was dead silent.

CHAPTER NINETEEN

The pain in his chest was so profound, he thought he was having a heart attack. The horror on her face sliced through him like a rusty blade ripping out his soul. In reality, his heart had broken.

Samantha squirmed from his grip. "Tell me what they said is a lie."

Dalton ran his hand through his hair, gripping and pulling until his they dropped to his side. "It's not what it seems." He moved toward her. She shuffled back until she hit the wall. Trapped, her eyes grew large, her face pale. She reminded him of an animal caught in a cage.

It gutted him to know she feared him when he'd never do anything to harm her. He loved her. Almost told her last night. Now he wished he would have because she'd never know the truth.

The one thing he'd always tried to be was the hero, and not the villain. He'd promised himself that his actions would never cause a woman to shake from terror, but Samantha was quaking like a leaf caught in a violent storm.

She slid down the wall like her bones had softened and could no longer hold her up. "Did you kill someone or not?" She didn't ask for details, just the facts.

"Yes."

"You need to leave." She scrambled back into the corner and curled into a ball.

"Please, Samantha, you have to listen to the facts."

"I need space," she yelled. "I need a minute to think."

"Dammit, would you listen to me?" He didn't mean to yell, but she had to give him a chance to explain.

"You know what my past is. You know I came from an abusive background. A man with a violent past is a deal breaker."

"I'm not that man." He dropped to his knees, feet from her, palms up so she wouldn't feel threatened. "I've never hit a woman. I lived in that environment too. I'm not my father. I'm not your father."

"How can you say that? You killed someone. They said a convicted killer."

He couldn't argue with her words or logic.

"Let me explain," he pleaded again.

She looked up at him with her soulful eyes, and all he saw was hurt and distrust.

"Now that it's out in the open, you want to explain? Why didn't you tell me?"

"We both kept truths from each other. Why are your omissions okay and mine aren't?"

The look of hurt fell away and was replaced by anger. He'd rather have her furious than afraid any day.

"You're right. We did. Let's say them out loud. I'm a pop star. You're a killer. How are those equal?" She laid her head on her knees. "Oh my God, the press will have a field day."

"Screw the press. This has nothing to do with them."

"Have you not heard a word I said? I'm a public figure."

He wanted to laugh at the hypocrisy of it all. "Until last night, you were in hiding. Why is that?"

"Because of stuff like this. I can't have a life."

He inched his way forward. "We had a good life until this morning. I'm not any different from the man who made love to you last night. It was love Samantha. Don't think for a second that you don't own my heart. That you haven't impacted me."

"This changes everything."

His shoulders sagged, and his arms dropped lifelessly next to his body. "It changes nothing."

When she chewed her lip for a minute, he knew there was still a chance. He only hoped she'd let him back in.

"Would you have pursued me if you'd known I was famous?"

Would he have? He wanted to be honest with her. "I would have fought my attraction to you because what happened out there is everything I don't want. I like my privacy. I like being invisible."

She laughed. Not the laugh that comes from a joke, but the laugh spurred on by disbelief. "Dalton, you're lying to yourself if you think you've ever been invisible."

"Well, it looks like we've both been lying to ourselves and to each other." He risked inching forward. If he saw any apprehension or fear in her body language, he'd move back, but he saw none.

"I lie to myself all the time." Her voice became whisper soft. "I tell myself that I love what I do. I tell myself that I can make it another year. I tell myself that I'll be fine." She burst into tears. "I'm not fine."

He couldn't stand the distance any longer. He moved closer and pulled her into his lap.

She curled into him. Maybe her grief was greater than her fear, but he loved how she clung to his body.

"Tell me more." He figured if he could get her talking, then maybe when she was finished, she'd be willing to listen.

"I love it here. For the first time in my life, I felt like I fit."

"Sweetheart, you fit." He pressed a kiss to the top of her head.

"It seems like I've been on the road for a decade. I'm tired, Dalton. I'm tired of being Indigo."

"Indigo isn't here; Samantha is, and she has a heart of gold. She's kind and forgiving. Last night, she let a stalker go free because she said everyone deserves a second chance." He lifted her chin so she had to look at him. "I'm part of everyone." He pulled her tight against his chest. "Give me a second chance."

She cried until his shirt was wet. "I'm sorry. You're right. Tell me your story."

He lifted her up and carried her to the couch. "I'll make some tea. Stay put." She nodded and tucked her tiny body into the corner. He pulled the soft throw she had folded over the arm and covered her.

While he was in the kitchen, he pulled his phone from his pocket and dialed the sheriff. "We've got a situation at Samantha's. We need to circle the wagons."

With two cups of tea ready, he returned. It crushed him to see her eyes red and swollen. He promised himself he'd stop at nothing to put a smile back on her face.

They sat in silence for minutes while he built up the courage to talk about a time he wished he could forget.

"Six years ago, I was in Denver at a bar called The Empty Keg. It's a dive bar, but it was close to school. On Fridays and Saturdays, the alcohol was cheap. I was playing pool with my buddies when I saw some guy grab a woman by the arm and drag her outside. They had been arguing off and on all night. He had been harassing her for attention. She ignored him. He didn't like the word no."

Dalton closed his eyes and relived the moment that changed his life.

"No one did anything. Everyone saw what was going on. It was obvious they weren't a couple. He'd been trying to pick her up all night, without luck." He opened his eyes and looked at Samantha, whose face was unreadable. "She fought him all the way out the door. She begged and pleaded for him to let her go. It was like listening to my mother when my father pulled her by her hair across the yard. I couldn't stand by and watch. I rushed out to help. By the time I got to her, he'd already punched her once. Told her she asked for it." He shook his head. "No woman asks for it." He set his tea down and tucked his fists under his legs. The replay always upset him. No matter how hard he tried, he could never come up with a different ending. "As the asshole wound up for another hit, I stepped in. He turned around and swung at me, connecting with my stomach. I hit him once. He never got back up."

When he looked at Samantha, fresh tears were running down her cheeks. Through a shaky voice, she asked, "You only hit him once?"

"That's all it took. Those six seconds got me six years in prison."

She set her cup down and pulled him close. It was time for her to comfort him. He was grateful for the gesture. She tugged and pulled at him until his head was in her lap.

"It sounds like self-defense." She ran her hand through his hair.

"That's what my lawyer pled, but a man was dead. There were lots of witnesses saying I hit him. No one saw him hit me."

"What about the girl?"

"She testified. It's probably why I got the minimum sentence." He remembered the judge's words verbatim. "A 'heat-of-passion' crime provoked by something that caused an ordinary person to become angry and act irrationally by killing someone." He let out a shaky breath and rubbed his head into her lap like a puppy craving attention.

"You gave me hints." She stroked his cheek with affection. "I'm so sorry I didn't listen."

"I'm sorry I didn't tell you right away. I thought about it, but everyone told me I shouldn't come out of the gate with 'I'm an ex-felon.'"

Despite the sorrow, she giggled. "That was probably wise counsel."

"We're both guilty of wanting someone to see us for who we are, and not who society has made us out to be."

"Where do we go from here?" she asked.

To bed, Dalton's inner voice screamed. If only they could go back an hour, he'd make love to her again and ignore the knock at the door. Despite the turn of events, he was relieved that the truth was finally out. Brutal as it was, he was still here with her. She wasn't shaking with fear but touching him with compassion.

This next part was going to kill him, but he knew it needed to be done. She came to Aspen Cove for clarity. She'd never get it if he was around. Their relationship was anything but clear. All he knew was that he wanted her, but he wouldn't keep her if it wasn't in her best interests.

She had a reputation to uphold. Last night when he'd looked up her music, he read more than once that she was America's sweetheart. The reporter's voice echoed in his head. *"Indigo! How do you think your fans will respond to your relationship with Dalton Black, a convicted killer?"* Samantha might be willing to forgive, but the press would never forget. He didn't want that for her. He didn't want it for himself.

He rolled to a sitting position. His body glued to her side. "You came here to get your thoughts straight. You wanted to find yourself. You won't be able to do that with all this noise around you." Her look of defeat told him he was right.

"I called the sheriff. He should get rid of the crowd."

"Thank you." She leaned her head on his chest and sighed.

"I'm going to leave you."

Her hands gripped his shirt like he was a lifeline. "I don't want to be alone."

"I don't want to leave you alone, but I know if I'm here, my presence won't give you the space you need to think and make sound decisions."

Her voice cracked with emotion. "I know you're right, but I hate it."

"I know I'm right, and for what it's worth, I hate it too. But I'll do it because I ... care."

He saw the words he wanted to say on her lips, She had fallen in love with him too, but he couldn't say them, or let her say them. If he heard the words or said them and couldn't have her, it would crush him. Instead, he pressed his lips softly to hers before he rose from the couch and went into the bedroom for his shoes.

When he came back, she was still sitting in the corner of the couch, staring into space.

"You're really leaving me?" Her wavering voice tugged at his heart.

"Not for good. Just for now." He pulled a smile from deep inside himself. "I'm free-birding you, baby."

She cocked her head. "You're what?"

"I'm letting you go. If you come back, I know it was meant to be." He pulled on his boots and put on his coat. "I texted the girls and told them you needed support."

She nodded. When he opened the front door, he saw that the press had been pushed back to the street. Sheriff Cooper walked toward him.

"You okay?"

"Not really." Dalton looked beyond him to where the reporters pulled long lenses from their bags.

"I can keep them off her property, not off the street. I'll send Mark over to keep an eye on things until it all settles down." He adjusted his hat and looked at the ground. "I looked her up. She's a big deal."

"She's everything."

CHAPTER TWENTY

The buzzing of her phone was relentless. Since only her mother and Deanna had the number, she had to look. She padded barefoot back to her room and sank onto her bed. Dalton's pillow cradled her head. It smelled like pine trees and pure man, like him.

She looked at the lit screen to see a dozen messages from Deanna all with the subject: **Trouble.**

Understatement. She pulled up her assistant's number and pressed call to connect. Deanna answered immediately.

"Oh. My. God. It's all over the news. Are you okay? Did they arrest him? Sweetie, it's not your fault."

"What?"

"The news said you were harboring a criminal." She heard the *tap tap* of a keyboard in the background. "Holy smokes. He's hot."

"They put his picture up?" She wanted to die right then. Not only had her career ruined her chance at a normal life, it had taken Dalton's peaceful existence away.

"Are you safe?"

"I was never in danger." Her stomach twisted from the guilt of cowering from him. The look on his face when she crawled into the corner of the room would slice her to pieces each time she remembered it. "It's not what it seems."

Those were his exact words, and she didn't listen to him. Why would anyone listen to her?

"We've got a lot of PR work to do. This is a huge mess. Dave Belton has called at least ten times in the last hour. I'm supposed to tell you you're in breach of contract. Something about protecting your image."

"Dave Belton can screw himself. He's all talk and no action."

Deanna let out a groan. "He's acting. He told me for each day you don't return, he's firing a member of your team."

Samantha shook her head to clear it. "How is that supposed to help? Let's say I come back next week. What do I come back to if my team is gone? Has he fired anyone else but you?"

Her silence was the answer. "Cohen got the ax thirty minutes ago."

"What?" Cohen was the best sound technician out there. "Hire him and give him a raise."

Deanna laughed. "Okay, but he doesn't get as much as me. He only gets ten percent."

"Fine." Her life was falling apart. She didn't need the extra bullshit Dave Belton was dishing out. She knew what his next game would be. He'd tell her how her career image was ruined, but if she stayed with him, he'd turn it all around.

"Are you coming back?"

The smart answer would have been yes, but the honest answer was no. "I can't. I'm not done here yet."

"You're in love with him, aren't you?"

Saying it out loud made it real. "Yes. He's not the man they say he is."

"I'm sorry I jumped to conclusions. The press rarely gets it right. You want me to put out a statement?"

"Not yet."

"Poor guy probably only has a parking ticket."

It wasn't funny, but Samantha couldn't stop the laughter bubbling inside her. "No, he killed someone."

"Okay, so you're in shock. A statement isn't probably wise. Have you distanced yourself?"

Samantha stood up and peeked between the cracks of the blinds of her bedroom window. Across the street, the paparazzi lay in wait. Unless she stayed a prisoner in her cabin, she would never get the peace and quiet she craved.

"He free-birded me."

"What? What does that mean?"

She walked through the house, pulling all the curtains and blinds closed. "Oh you know, that crap about loving someone and setting them free."

"I'm confused. He's a killer, but you love him anyway. He loves you, but because you're a rich, sexy pop star, he let you go?"

"Something like that." Samantha gave Deanna a shortened version of Dalton's story.

"Oh ..." Deanna's said with a dreamy voice. "I may be in love with him too."

"Find your own felon. He's mine." She'd come to Aspen Cove to find something. She thought it was clarity, but the only thing she was clear about was how much she loved Dalton Black.

A soft knock sounded at the door.

"I have to go."

"Wait, is there anything else I can do?"

"Make sure my band and crew know they have jobs. Other than that, keep an eye out about what people are posting. I refuse to let my fame ruin a good man."

"Got it, Boss."

On the next round of knocks, Samantha peeked out the peephole to see Sage, Katie, and baby Sahara on her doorstep.

She opened it a crack and disappeared behind the door so the press wouldn't snap her photo while her friends entered.

"Thanks for coming. I hope I didn't take you away from anything."

"You saved me. Doc can deal with that case of hemorrhoids by himself. No one should see that before lunch." Sage opened her purse and took out candy bar after candy bar. She picked up the peanut butter cups and handed them to Samantha. "These are particularly helpful in a time of crisis."

Samantha took the candy gratefully. She'd been shaking for the last half an hour. It could have been nerves or low blood sugar. "What about you?" She looked at Katie. "Shouldn't you be at the bakery?"

Katie walked over to the chair by the couch and sat down. Her diaper bag fell on the floor. She reached inside and took out a box of muffins. "That's the beauty of owning something. No one can tell you what, when, or how to do anything. Besides, Ben was happy to take over."

Sage and Samantha took positions on opposite ends of the couch.

Sage leaned in and looked at Samantha closely. "Yep, you're her. I didn't recognize you without the blue hair."

Katie pulled a bottle from her bag to feed Sahara. "I knew right away. Why do you think I saddled her with that song on karaoke night?"

"Which, by the way, you killed," Sage added. "Every man in that room envied Dalton."

"Is anyone looking after Dalton?" Samantha knew he was trying to protect her, but who was protecting him?

"He took off on his bike," Katie said. "He's a private person. He needed to get away."

"From me." That blade of guilt cut deeper, making her hemorrhage inside.

"He'd never leave you unless he thought it was what was best for you." Katie lifted the baby to her shoulder and patted her back until she released a belch twice as big as she was. "She burps like her daddy."

"Why does everyone think they know what's best for me? When do I get to choose for myself?" That fire of fury burned inside her. All her life her choices were taken away. First by an abusive father that kept her mother and her on the run for years. Next it was her manager, who thought he could strong-arm her into submission. Now it was Dalton, who walked out of her life because he thought it best.

"Choose now and choose us." Sage took the peanut butter cups from Samantha. "If you're not going to eat these, I will." She tore open the wrapper and hummed at the first bite.

Samantha threw her hands into the air. "Will life ever be easy?"

Katie passed Sahara to Sage and stood in front of Samantha, where she pulled her T-shirt up to reveal a scar that ran the length of her chest. "Not easy, but worth it." She flopped back into her seat and told Samantha her story. She covered everything from her illness to her donor heart to Bowie, and then Sahara. "If you want it, you have to fight for it. Sometimes you have to take scary steps to get what you want."

Samantha wanted to crawl under the couch with the dust bunnies—she felt as useless as one. "I asked him to leave before he explained. He wouldn't leave. He fought for me."

"Will you fight for him?" Katie asked.

Would she? "Without a doubt—but then what happens to us? We have such different lives."

Sage bounced the chubby baby on her knee. "You think Cannon and I were anything alike? Opposites attract, and if you don't kill each other falling in love, it's a beautiful thing."

"I'm such an idiot."

"Only if you let someone amazing slip away," Sage said.

"You guys have to go."

They both looked at her in surprise.

"You want us to leave?" Katie asked.

"I'm texting Dalton. If you want to be here when I ask him to forgive me and take me to bed, then you can stay. If not you should go, but before you do, I want to tell you both how much I value your friendship and advice." Samantha rolled to her feet and hugged both of them before she herded them toward the door.

The paparazzi snapped pictures right away. This time, Samantha didn't hide behind the door or her friends. It was time to fight. She stepped out with Sage and Katie, who looked at each other and laughed before they gave the press the bird.

She leaned over the rail and pointed to the only reporter she recognized and told him to come forward. He looked at her with skepticism. Sitting to the side of her house was the deputy sheriff.

She walked to the cruiser and told him she needed to see one particular reporter. He exited his SUV and escorted the man to her.

"What's up, Indigo?"

"Ray, you've always been fair to me. If I give you an exclusive interview, will you continue to be fair to me? Most importantly, you need to be fair to Dalton."

"You're going to give me an exclusive?"

"Yes."

"Do you know how famous that will make me?"

"Be careful, fame isn't all it's cracked up to be."

"Can I quote you?"

"Yes." Wasn't it time to be honest with herself and everyone around her? Her statement would anger many people. Most would trade their lives for hers. She'd trade everything she had for another night with Dalton. "I'll call you when I'm ready to talk."

He fished for a card from his pocket. "I can't wait."

"Neither can I." She wasn't talking about the interview. She was talking about seeing Dalton again.

She went back inside and picked up her phone to text a message.

Dalton,

I've made a lot of mistakes in my life, but the

biggest was letting you walk out that door. Please come home. I miss you. I miss the gray.

With love,

Samantha

She set down the phone and raced to the bathroom so she was showered and ready when he came back. If he came back.

CHAPTER TWENTY-ONE

Dalton zipped toward Silver Springs on his Harley. He would have gone to Copper Creek, but it was too close and held fresh memories of his time with Samantha. Besides, he couldn't be certain he wouldn't end up at Chachi's, ready to wring Todd's neck. That little asshole was responsible for this whole shit show. Without a doubt, he posted her picture and disclosed her location.

The crisp mountain air whipped around him as he drove too fast through the pass. Carelessness outweighed caution. His phone vibrated inside his pocket. He ignored it while he weaved between cars, taking risks that could kill him. He realized how stupidly he'd behaved. His death wouldn't solve anything except possibly the ache in his chest since he walked out of Samantha's cabin. He wasn't sure he could go back to his status quo when he'd been given a taste of heaven.

Besides, it would break his mom's heart if he died. He knew his friends well enough to know they'd bring him back to life so they could kill him again for his stupidity.

The driver in front of him slammed on her brakes to avoid hitting a deer. He averted disaster by a hair when he swerved right and missed eating the back end of the midsize sedan by inches. Sadly, he caught his tire on the soft shoulder and down he went. The fall wouldn't kill him, but it would hurt like a bastard.

The denim of his jeans tore as he slid across the asphalt. The loose gravel bit into his skin. His Harley, with the momentum of a freight train, sped ahead of him, hit the guardrail, and flipped over the edge. The sound of metal crashed and crumbled as his prized possession flew over the cliff and tumbled down the embankment.

Dalton came to rest on his back near the metal rail. He took a mental and physical inventory. He could move both legs, both arms, and all his fingers. His head was still attached and safely inside his helmet until he unbuckled the strap and tossed it aside. Once he knew he'd survived, the pain kicked in. His entire left side was on fire from his ankle to his hip. Thankfully, he'd worn his leather jacket, or else the road rash would have claimed more real estate on his body.

"Are you okay?" An older woman rushed to his aid. "You were tailing too close. I almost hit the deer. You almost hit me."

She rattled off facts he couldn't deny. He'd been tailing her.

"I'm fine. It's a scratch." He glanced down at his blood-soaked, shredded jeans and groaned.

"That's more than a scratch."

"I'll be all right." He pulled himself up to a sitting position and leaned against the cold metal barrier.

She peeked over the edge where his bike had taken flight. Her eyes grew big, and her face blanched almost as white as her hair. "You're in better shape than that death mobile. I'll never understand the attraction to motorcycles. You don't see people riding on the outside of planes, do you? It's not safe."

He didn't want to argue with her, but in early aviation lots of people flew without being encased in tons of metal. After a closer look, he was pretty certain she'd been alive when the Wright brothers took their first flight.

"Yes, ma'am. I'm sorry I scared you. I'm all right." A few snowflakes dropped from the sky. "Great. Just great." He leaned back and thunked his head on the metal. Until that point, it was the only thing that didn't ache.

"You need a doctor."

"I've got one." He knew if he showed up to Doc's like this, the old man would skin what hadn't been skinned already.

"My name is Agatha Guild." She pulled on his arm to help him stand. "I'll give you a ride. What's your name?"

"I'm Dalton, and I'm okay. I'll call for help."

"Oh fiddlesticks, you young ones can be so stubborn. I'm taking you home." She yanked and pulled until he had no choice but to comply or have his arm ripped from the socket. For being an antique, she was quite strong, and Dalton feared he'd lose a limb if she kept tugging.

He managed to stand. The pain of the fall sliced through him. Each step he took was worse than the last. Bits of dirt and gravel rubbed against the denim and dug deeper into his skin.

"Really, I can call a friend."

"Dalton whoever you are ... I don't want any lip from you." She led him to her car and opened the trunk. "I don't want you bleeding everywhere."

Dalton's head shook slowly back and forth. "Agatha, I'm not riding in your trunk."

"Of course not." She leaned in and grabbed a blanket. "Are you sure you didn't hit your head?" She covered the upholstery of the front passenger seat. He climbed inside. "Where are we going?" She buckled in and adjusted her seat. She was a tiny thing, much like Samantha, only Ms. Guild could barely see over the steering wheel.

"I live in Aspen Cove."

"You don't say." She pulled a U-turn and headed in the opposite direction she had been traveling. "Your doctor wouldn't happen to be Doctor Parker, would it?"

"You know him?"

"Oh, yes," she said, all dreamy. "I know him. He was my square dancing partner last year."

"Doc square dances?"

She smiled. "A man of many talents."

Maybe he imagined it, but Ms. Guild seemed to imply she'd been the recipient of his talents. Then again, Dalton's body hurt so bad, he wasn't thinking clearly. He imagined a lot of things, like the smell of chocolate chip cookies and the sound of Samantha's voice telling him to come home.

He remembered the vibration in his pocket prior to the crash and pulled out his phone. There was one text message. It was from Samantha.

Dalton,

I've made a lot of mistakes in my life, but the biggest was letting you walk out that door. Please come home. I miss you. I miss the gray.

With love,

Samantha

Her message gutted him. He wanted to race back to her, but he wasn't racing anywhere. Agatha Guild drove thirty in a fifty, which was why he was riding her ass in the first place. At least that's the lie he told himself. He knew if she were going eighty, he would have still been on her tail. All he wanted to do was gain distance from the situation and the pain, not from Samantha.

He thought about what he could say to her when he saw her again. He wanted to make this better, but the facts were the facts: He was an ex-felon. She was a pop star. There would never be a place for him in her life as long as the public continued to try him. The hardest thing to do was to let her go. The kindest thing to do was to let her go. He had to let her go.

Samantha,

We had the beginning. We had the end. I wish we'd had more of the in-between. Take care of yourself. Be true to yourself.

With love,

Dalton

He hovered over the send button. When he pressed it, his heart hollowed out. He leaned his forehead on the window and watched the pine trees pass until the glass fogged and everything seemed hazy. They crawled toward Aspen Cove. The closer they got, the heavier the snow fell and the slower Agatha drove. Outside of the need to ease the pain in his leg, it didn't matter when they arrived. There was nothing to rush toward.

"Almost there." Agatha pulled in front of Doc's clinic. "Stay here."

For an old woman, she moved faster on her feet than she did on the road. Not wanting Doc or Sage to rush a gurney out to him, he exited the car and hobbled into the building.

The first person he saw was Sage, who helped him to the examination room. He limped past Doc and Agatha, who were exchanging niceties. Agatha blushed when Doc Parker told her he'd call her.

"What happened?" Sage rushed around the room, pulling out scissors and tweezers and a metal pan.

"I'm not pissing in that."

She laughed. "Wouldn't think of asking you to. It's for saline. We have to clean out the wounds."

"Agatha said you were flirting with death." Doc walked in and washed his hands. He made quick work of cutting off Dalton's jeans. "Flirting with pretty little brunettes would be a better choice."

"Like you were flirting with Agatha?" Dalton tried to tease through his pain.

He let out a curse when Doc peeled the denim from his wound. He looked down and saw what looked like ground beef.

"You could be with Samantha if you weren't sitting here." Doc yanked another piece of denim loose.

Anyone who said quick was painless was full of shit. Dalton sucked in a fortifying breath before he replied, "Obviously, you haven't heard the news."

"Heard it. Can't say I liked it. They got it all wrong."

Dalton hissed as Doc flushed the abraded skin with saline, then went to work with the tweezers. "Dammit Doc, do you have to dig to my spleen?"

Doc turned to Sage. "Make the necessary calls."

Dalton tried to rise from the table. "Don't call anyone." He didn't want anyone to make a big deal out of this. The faster he could become invisible, the better. He couldn't be invisible if Sage sent out the 4-1-1 on his 9-1-1.

Doc's cuff to the side of his head was swift and uncomfortable. He still had great reflexes for an old fart. "You don't get to make the rules inside my clinic." He jabbed a little deeper and came out with a pebble that pinged when it hit the metal pan.

He glanced at Sage and shook his head, hoping she'd heed his request. "Really, Sage, I'll be fine."

His plea fell on deaf ears as she left the room.

"Agatha says your bike is at the bottom of a ravine. Trying to kill yourself?"

"No, trying to put some space between me and the press."

"Now, listen here, son."

Dalton groaned. "I'm all ears."

"It's about the only thing you have left. Too bad you're not using what's between them." Doc found a rhythm, and the ping of pebbles in the pan became the backdrop to his lesson. "Do you like her?"

"Samantha? What's not to like?"

"Did you tell her about your past?" Doc dropped the tweezers into the basin and flushed Dalton's injury with more saline.

"She heard it from the press first."

"And?"

"After I explained, it was okay."

"I knew I liked that girl."

"Don't you get it? We can't be together. We knew going in there was an expiration date."

"You're wrong. The only true expiration date is sour milk and death. The rest is logistics."

"We come from different worlds."

Doc slathered soothing salve on the raw skin and wrapped gauze around Dalton's leg from ankle to hip. He tugged tight for emphasis. Not because he needed to but because he wanted Dalton's attention.

"Puppy brains." He shook his head. "She comes from your world. You think she came here to be Indigo?" Doc reached into the cabinet and pulled out a pair of scrub pants. "She came here to find herself again. Go show her who she is and show the world who you are." When Dalton opened his mouth to argue, Doc pulled a cherry Life Saver from his pocket and popped it into Dalton's mouth. "Get dressed. I think I hear your mother coming."

As he struggled into the pair of scrubs, his mother burst through the door. Ben, Sage, Bowie, Cannon, and Katie, carrying Sahara, followed her. Dalton craned his neck to see if Samantha came after. She didn't. Why would she? They were no longer a thing.

Disappointment filled his empty heart. After everyone reprimanded him for his carelessness, Cannon led him outside to his truck.

"Sheriff Cooper called in some favors. The Silver Springs Police Department is going to get what's left of your bike." They drove down Main Street to Lake Circle, but instead of turning right toward Dalton's cabin, Cannon pulled up close to the steps in front of the bed and breakfast.

"What are you doing? Just take me home."

"No can do. I've been given directions from Sage. Do you have any idea what kind of trouble I'd be in if I didn't follow instructions?"

"You're so whipped." Dalton looked around before he climbed slowly out of the truck. He didn't want to attract unwanted publicity to the bed and breakfast.

Cannon looked past him. "They're still camped out in front of Samantha's cabin. They can't see you here."

It seemed an accurate statement. If he couldn't see them because of the bend in the road, then most likely they wouldn't see him. "Is she okay? Is she safe?"

"*Okay* is a relative term, but she's safe."

Dalton limped up the steps.

"Why am I here?" He stepped into the unusually darkened room. In the shadows, a silhouette moved in his direction.

"Because I needed to see you." Samantha rushed to him and wrapped her arms around his waist. She filled the cold, cavernous hole in his heart with her warmth and presence.

CHAPTER TWENTY-TWO

"What were you thinking?" She stepped back to take inventory of him. When Sage called and said Dalton had laid his bike down on the highway, she'd nearly had heart failure. She'd only just found him. There was no way she was losing him.

"I'm fine." He limped forward and cupped her cheek. "Better now that you're here. I'm so sorry."

Cannon cleared his throat behind them. "That would be my cue to leave." He backed up toward the door. "Sage says the last guest room is yours to use. She also said she'd bring home dinner."

Samantha and Dalton tried to stifle their groans, but it was hard to silence the sound of terror. "Man, I need to teach that woman how to cook."

Cannon laughed. "Been there, tried that. What we need is one of those places that sells prepared meals for the busy family."

Samantha's eyes brightened in the dim light. "That's a brilliant idea. I wonder if there are enough people in Aspen Cove to keep it open?" She imagined the town could figure it out. They managed to keep a bakery, a bar, and a diner in business.

Cannon left them alone. They stood in the middle of the living room, staring at each other.

"Let's get you to bed." Samantha led Dalton down the hallway. He moved slowly, favoring his left side. He inched onto the bed and sighed when he was settled.

"How did you get here without being seen?" He shifted to his right to get comfortable. His left side was on fire. She could feel the heat rising from his skin.

"Katie choreographed it all. She contacted the sheriff, who had his deputy distract the reporters while I snuck out the back door. Real cloak-and-dagger kind of stuff." She laughed at how she'd hunkered down and ran from cabin to cabin until she cleared the deck and dove inside the opened back door to the bed and breakfast. Cannon closed the blinds, and she waited and worried. "If you weren't already shredded to pieces, I'd skin you alive myself. You left me."

"I'm sorry. I was trying to protect you. I still want to protect you."

Samantha climbed onto the bed and curled up next to his body. She was careful to stay away from the left side he favored. "I know, and I love that you wanted to save me. I can't remember a time when anyone gave up something for me, but I don't want you to give me up to save me. I don't want to give you up."

"You know you can't keep me. You've said so yourself."

"What if I could? Would you want me to?"

He wrapped his arm around her and tugged her tight against his chest. "Yes. I'll always want you."

She tilted her face toward his, and he kissed her softly and slowly. A lingering kiss that said he was happy to see her.

"We'll figure it out." She had no idea how it could work, but she had to find a way. She knew the press would hound her. They would also hound him. That's what worried her the most. She'd signed up for it. He hadn't.

His past and his presence could ruin her career. Maybe it already had. The headlines were full of stories and pictures. The latest one was of her and Sage and Katie giving the press the finger. Right next to it was Dalton's mug shot, but she cared less about her career than she did about his privacy.

"You need to rest." She reached for the quilt folded at the foot of the bed. He hissed as she pulled it over him. "I'm sorry. How bad is it?"

"I'll survive."

"What can I do to ease your pain?" Her hand ran up and down his chest until it settled on the waistband of the scrubs Doc had sent him home in.

His beautiful blue eyes turned from blue to a stormy, gunmetal gray. "Don't tease an injured man."

Her hand slipped below the elastic band and stroked the length of him. "Maybe if I made you feel good somewhere else, you'd forget how much you actually hurt." When he opened his mouth, she gripped him tighter. Instead of a rebuttal, she got the sweet moan of pleasure.

"Let me make you feel better, Dalton. Let me take your pain away, if only for a minute." She didn't wait for permission. She carefully inched his pants down and gasped at the extent of his injuries. Gauze covered him from hip to ankle. "Oh honey, I had no idea it was this bad." Her fingers skimmed the bandage. "Maybe I shouldn't touch you."

"Please," he begged. "Touch me." He lifted his hips. "Samantha. Touch me."

She started at his lips and kissed her way down his body. She wasn't sure if it was the wisest thing to do, but his throaty hum of pleasure told her it was the best thing to do. Hovering over his silky hard length, her tongue darted out for a taste.

"Christ, Samantha." He let out a long, shaky breath and stilled.

"Shh. Let me love you." His body was hot, hard, and ready.

Dalton didn't speak. He didn't move. He gripped the bedspread in his hands and held on for the ride.

She stroked him with the heat of her mouth. Taking as much of him in before she hummed a song.

Dalton released a low and throaty groan that was so sexy, it made her body quiver to give him such pleasure. As he tensed beneath her touch, she increased the pressure, quickened the pace. His hands threaded through her hair, guiding her where he wanted her.

She looked up to see his eyes closed and a look of pure pleasure on his face. His breath quickened, and his muscles tensed.

"Samantha, I'm—" He tried to pull her away. He sank his hips deeper into the mattress.

She ignored him and continued until her efforts wrenched a groan. His muscles tensed, then shook, and he came with a curse. She didn't let up until his body finished shuddering and his muscles relaxed.

He reached for her and pulled her up and next to him. "God, Samantha. That was ... everything."

Samantha knew the sentiment well. Each time Dalton loved her body, it was everything. She feared without him, she'd have nothing.

"I'm sorry I left you. I really thought I was doing the right thing."

"Dalton, we are stronger together." Samantha curled into his side until she heard his breath deepen and slow. When she knew he was asleep, she rolled out of bed and sat in the chair in the corner with her phone.

Deanna had been texting her regularly throughout the day. Each hour, she'd sent a message with the name of the newest sacrificial lamb. Dave was firing a person an hour. Samantha was hiring a person per hour. By the end of the day, she'd have her own crew. All she needed was a label and a recording studio.

The next hour, she traded messages with her accountant. He wasn't pleased with the turn of events, but he wasn't a fan of Dave's, so he understood her need to protect those loyal to her.

She dozed for a minute, dreaming about a future that didn't seem possible. In the dream, she and Dalton walked hand in hand down Main Street. It was spring, and her friends peeked their faces out of the shops to say hello. Children played in Hope Park. Businesses moved into the Guild. It was perfect until she woke up and realized it was a dream. The beauty of dreams was, they cost nothing and anything was possible.

Dalton stirred, and she rushed to his side, climbing onto the bed to snuggle next to him. "You okay? You need anything?"

He wrapped his free arm around her. "I've got everything I need."

FOR THREE DAYS, they hid out at the bed and breakfast. No one was the wiser that Dalton had returned to Aspen Cove or that Samantha had left her cabin. Sage and Katie pretended to visit each day. They'd stay a few minutes and bring clean clothes. Bowie made a middle-of-the-night visit to Dalton's and picked up a few things he needed.

Three beautiful, blissful days were spent in each other's arms. It was like putting her life on pause while they caught up. It was easy to get to know a person when you spent every minute of every day with them. She liked what he did for her body, but she loved what he did for her soul. She'd come to Aspen Cove to find clarity. For those hours Dalton was gone, nothing was clear. The minute he returned, it came together. She may have had it all, but she had nothing without him.

Come Sunday, they had to vacate their room at the bed and breakfast. Sage had a group arriving that afternoon. Samantha and Dalton braved the world together. What was done was done. She was getting a lot of backlash from her relationship with Dalton, but if she let society decide who she could date, she was no better off than when she allowed Dave to be a dictator.

She had heard nothing from him in two days, which was simultaneously nice and terrifying. Dave was not the type of man to go down easy.

Dalton was stiff and sore, but each day he moved more fluidly. At night when he made love to her, she couldn't even tell he was injured.

They looked outside. They had two choices: They could walk proudly out the front door and up the street into the throng of persistent reporters, or they could sneak back along the edge of the water to their cabins. Samantha decided their path when she said she would not hide the best thing in her life.

Hand in hand, they left the bed and breakfast and walked down Lake Circle. About a half dozen photographers turned in shock to see the couple appear. Shutters clicked, and the questions came nonstop.

When they reached the front of Dalton's cabin, Samantha's heart dropped to the hard ground. Spray painted in red over the exterior of his cabin was the word 'Killer'.

She turned toward the reporters. "Where were your cameras when this was going on?" She stomped forward until she was in front of Jake. "I expected more from you. You have a responsibility to report the truth. Report the damn truth, and do it with fairness and integrity." Her voice rose until it hit near hysteria. She pointed to Dalton, and then looked back at the reporters. "He killed a man, and by definition that makes him a killer, but do your damn homework. He's not a killer. He's the best man I know."

She marched toward Dalton and threaded her fingers through his in a sign of unity. "My house or yours?"

"Mine. I'll make you an edible meal." She followed him inside. The cameras clicked, and she knew the next picture posted would be of her and Dalton walking into his home, beside them the red paint, running down the wood like blood.

In minutes, Dalton was in the kitchen whipping together a meal worthy of Michelin's highest three-star rating. Samantha set the table. They sat in front of the window overlooking the lake. Days ago the water was solid, but today cracks and fissures marred the once smooth surface, proving that everything changed.

"In a few weeks, you won't even know the lake was ever covered in ice." Dalton poured them a glass of white wine and sat down next to her to enjoy the salmon and grilled veggies.

"Hopefully in a few weeks, all of this other stuff will be a memory too." Samantha laid her hand on top of Dalton's. "I'll get someone to fix your house."

"It's not a big deal." Though his words were positive, the lines on his face were etched with concern.

She sipped her wine. Actually gulped it. She needed the alcohol to numb her anger. Name-calling was one thing. Destroying someone's property was another. Why did his crime count and the vandal's didn't?

"It's a big deal to me. If I wouldn't have come here, your life wouldn't have changed."

He dropped his fork, and his tight expression softened with such love and passion. "If you hadn't come here, Samantha, my life *wouldn't have changed.*"

"Yes, that's what I said." She picked up her glass and emptied it.

"Change isn't always a bad thing."

"I don't want to be bad for you." She forked a bite of perfectly cooked fish.

"Baby, you're so bad, you're good."

"Get me drunk, and I'll show you how bad I can be."

He topped off her glass.

CHAPTER TWENTY-THREE

Dalton left his house early in the morning. Thankfully, the paparazzi weren't early risers. The only cameras present belonged to the reporters sleeping in their cars. In his rearview mirror, he watched as the red paint on his house faded from sight.

Not wanting to cause his mom or his business problems, he snuck into the kitchen from the back entrance and went to work. He liked to visit their patrons, but he knew he'd be stuck in the kitchen all day.

When his mother walked in, she did what all good mothers do. She wrapped her arms around him and gave him a hug. It was the same hug she'd given him seven years ago after sentencing, and the same hug she gave him last year when he came home. The hug that said, "I love you unconditionally, and I wish I could improve your life."

No words were exchanged. They didn't need words. It was always them against the world, and both knew they had each other's back.

Maisey stood back. "How's the road rash?"

"Feels better than it looks." He'd inspected the scabbing after his shower. There were a few deep places where he'd scar, but all in all, considering he'd slid about fifty feet across the pavement, he was in good shape.

"How is Samantha?" Maisey had visited them in the bed and breakfast several times. Dalton wasn't sure if it was to spend time with him and Samantha or save them from frozen lasagna, because she always came with food. One night it was chicken fried chicken with mashed potatoes and gravy. The second time, it was spaghetti and meatballs, the kind that simmered on a stovetop for hours.

"She's good. Her life is a mess. Her manager is a jerk. The press continues to hound her. They're trying her for my crime."

"She seems tough enough to handle it all."

"For a tiny thing, she's filled with tough stuff. I worry that my presence in her life will ruin her career. Fans are fickle."

Mom prepped several coffee filters, filling them with grounds and stacking them up so they were ready when she opened the door. One positive thing about the influx of press was that it would bring more customers to the diner. So far, no one had put two and two together and figured out that Dalton was Maisey's son. She was a Bishop now, and that would help. Plus, they were too focused on Samantha and Dalton to give other family connections much thought.

He hated that one act years ago would define his life forever and possibly ruin the lives of those he loved.

"I like her, Dalton. It takes courage to be the one percent."

Samantha was part of the 'one percent' that saw him for the man he was, and not the man the press made him out to be.

"I like her too." He liked everything about her, from the way he fit inside her body to the way she sang when no one was looking. Those were the songs from her heart. She spent hours each day curled up next to him, scribbling on a notepad. She said she was writing her next album and that it would be a secret.

Maisey took the stack of prepped coffee filters and walked through the swinging doors. It was seven o'clock and time to open.

Business was booming. Dalton didn't have time to slow down

until the doors closed at two. He was scraping the grill when the back door opened and Samantha walked inside.

"How did you get away?"

"The sheriff came and got me. He said he had some errands to run and thought I might like lunch. He told the reporters that if they followed him, he'd cite them for interfering with an investigation. When they asked him what kind of investigation, he spouted off a dozen things that started with invasion of privacy to slander. They packed up their bags and left. If I wasn't there, there was no story. I'm sure they'll be back."

"Are you hungry?" Dalton lifted her and set her down on the stainless-steel prep table. He stepped between her legs and pressed a soft kiss to her lips. "I can make you that omelet you like. Or how about a waffle?"

"I hoped you could start your culinary school and make me your first student."

"You want to learn how to cook?"

"I want to learn how to cook something you like to eat."

Dalton's mind went straight to the gutter. His hands traveled up the thighs of her worn jeans and settled at the juncture between. "My favorite thing to eat requires absolutely no prep. The only ingredient is you."

"Men." She shook her head. "One-track mind. Besides, that's dessert." She winked at him and slid from the metal table to the tile floor. She wrapped her arms around his waist. He expected her to squeeze him tight like she always did. Instead, she removed his apron and tied it around her waist.

"Your student is ready."

He laughed. The hem of his apron reached the tops of her tennis shoes. "You're going to trip." He rolled it up and retied it to her waist. "Can you boil water?"

She fisted up and slugged him in the arm. "I'm not Sage. I've got water boiling down to an art. I can also make a mean grilled cheese and an awesome mystery loaf."

"Mystery loaf?"

She smiled. "Like you, when I was a kid, I did some cooking. Mom worked all day, so I made dinner, but I was limited to three things. It was cheesy potato and ham casserole, meatloaf or what I called mystery loaf because I tossed in whatever we had, or grilled cheese. I can't say I mastered any of them, but grilled cheese was the best. The rest, I mostly ruined." Her shoulders slumped forward. "I'm good at ruining things."

He lifted her chin and kissed her sweetly. "Not everything."

The sound that left her was a cross between a snort and a groan. "Look at your life now. Two weeks ago you were living a happy, quiet life, and now everything is a mess."

"Sweetheart, two weeks ago I wasn't even living. I didn't know it until you arrived."

She pulled a hair tie from her pocket and fastened her hair into a high ponytail. "You can't say it's been boring. I mean, I've brought *a lot* to Aspen Cove." She said it in a tongue-in-cheek fashion. "There's the pestilence that camps outside our cabins." She walked around the kitchen, checking out the spices, the equipment, and him.

He nodded. "There's that."

"I sang you a song or two." She hummed something he didn't recognize.

Dalton thought about how much he liked her humming when her mouth was full—of him. "I like it when you sing." He reached above the grill for a loaf of bread.

"And we can't forget about the art."

He placed the bread on the counter and pulled a block of cheese from the refrigerator below. "The art?"

She opened her eyes and tilted her head. "I like the band The Killers, but I wouldn't have chosen to spray paint it on my cabin."

He laughed even though it wasn't funny. No one wanted to live in a place that was vandalized in such a way. "No accounting for taste."

"Speaking of taste, what are you going to teach me to cook?"

"I thought we'd learn from each other. You teach me how to make a mean grilled cheese sandwich, and I'll teach you how to make roasted creamy tomato soup from scratch."

They went to work side by side. Her secret recipe was to throw in several varieties of cheese, and instead of butter, she slathered the bread with mayonnaise and cooked it to a golden brown. Dalton fire roasted several tomatoes, added them to the blender with stock and cream and a few spices.

Fifteen minutes later, they were sitting in the diner with Maisey and Ben eating the best grilled cheese sandwich of his life with passable tomato soup. In a perfect world, this would be his forever. Sadly, the world was imperfect, but not in that moment.

Once the kitchen was cleaned, they piled into his truck. They didn't return home right away because going back to the cabin meant ruining this perfect moment, so they headed to the other side of the lake to visit Sam and eat ice cream.

Today's flavors were Bee's Knees, with honeycomb chunks and mini chocolate chips; Bloody Sundae, with vanilla ice cream and raspberry sauce; and Monkey in the Middle, with chocolate ice cream with bananas. Sam sprinkled them all with his 'ants'.

Samantha sat on Dalton's right side, afraid she'd bump into his left and hurt him. He loved the way she looked out for him even though all thoughts of his injuries were gone the second they hit the sheets.

They finished their ice cream, and he helped her into the truck when his phone buzzed. Cannon messaged him and told him to pull between their cabins and park on the lakeside of his property.

"I think the press is back in full force." He handed his phone to Samantha.

She read the text and groaned. "I'm so sorry. Maybe I should leave."

Before he started the truck, he turned in her direction. "You are not leaving me. We'll figure it all out. Eventually, they'll get bored and leave us alone."

She raised her perfectly plucked brow like she didn't believe him. He had to get her to believe because he wanted her to stay.

"I didn't come to Aspen Cove to ruin the town."

He unbuckled her seat belt and pulled her to his side. "How have you ruined anything?" She straddled his lap, and he bit back a groan when her shoe scraped along the deepest part of his injured leg. "You make everything sweeter." He kissed her passionately and pulled back. "You are the Bee's Knees."

She touched her forehead to his. "That's the ice cream you're tasting."

"Doubtful. I've tasted you and the ice cream. You are infinitely more satisfying."

"Remember that when something else goes wrong."

He cupped her frowning face. "Samantha, life will never be easy. I knew that before I met you, but you make whatever we have to face worthwhile. We are better together." They sat in the truck for another five minutes and held each other. They were enjoying their time together or maybe getting the courage to face what was to come.

When they arrived back in Aspen Cove, things weren't as he expected. Gone was the word 'Killers'. In front of his cabin was Wes Covington, the town's resident contractor. He stood in front of the newly sandblasted cabin, winding up the cord to his equipment. Dalton waved as he passed.

Samantha turned her head and watched the reporters run for cover.

"Are those bees?"

In front of his cabin was Abby Garrett in full beekeeping gear, setting up her hives.

One thing he loved about the town was how the locals circled the wagons around their own.

CHAPTER TWENTY-FOUR

"Bees?" Deanna said. "Your security system is bees?"

"That's right," Samantha replied. She took a diet soda from the refrigerator and walked to the front door, where she watched Abby shake bees from the hive. Swarms of them flew in every direction. The last of the diehard photographers took off running. "It's quite effective."

"Are you doing okay? I know it's been crazy."

Samantha popped the top of the can and listened to the hiss of carbonation escape. 'Crazy' didn't begin to describe the past week.

Whirlwind.

Fabulous.

Terrifying.

Heartbreaking.

There were a hundred words that could describe the past week. 'Crazy' was not the one she'd choose. "I don't know. It's been hard to watch Dalton get dragged through the court of public opinion. He's been great through it all. Keeps telling me that what we have is bigger than what anyone can throw at us, but I'm worried he'll change his mind."

"He sounds like a good man. Seems to have a handle on it. Don't worry. He'll let you know if it's too much."

Samantha walked away from the front door to the back of the house, where the windows faced the lake. She wished she could open the blinds and enjoy the view. The ice on the lake was melting, and the water had lapped up onto the shore. It made a soft, comforting swish she wished she could hear, but she'd seen more than one reporter ignore the sheriff's warning and sneak behind the cabin on the unlikely chance they'd get a sellable shot. Maybe they simply avoided the sting of Abby's bees.

"I'm not sure he would tell me. Look at what he's been through. Compared to prison, I'm sure everything is bearable. I don't want to be someone he has to bear."

"Believe me, there are days when you are unbearable." Deanna's laughter filled the phone. "Show me a day when I can't sneak you a piece of chocolate, and I'll show you unbearable."

"Now you're being mean."

Deanna sighed. "No ... mean is trying to cancel the benefit concert because the sponsor is stupid."

Samantha sank into the soft leather of her couch. "No. Tell me they're not trying to cancel it." She couldn't believe the Domestic Abuse Co-op would give up the hundreds of thousands of dollars the concert would pull in.

The silence on Deanna's end said it all. "It's not a firm no. We're talking about the potential to lose lots of money here. As you know, money talks, but they aren't happy with Mr. Black's background. Something about a pop star who's in love with a violent man can't be the poster child against domestic abuse."

"He's not that guy. If they could only meet him. He's kind and loving and—"

"I know, a good kisser among other things. Where is the hottie now?" Deanna had been sending Samantha all the pictures the press had taken and posted. She couldn't argue with her. Dalton Black was one handsome man. He even looked good in prison orange. Like

Indigo, he had that bad-boy image, but inside he was as sweet as Sam's Scoops ice cream.

"He worked all morning, so he went home to shower and change. He's coming back later to binge watch *Supernatural* with me."

"You're killing me. You have the hottest man I've ever seen in your cabin, and you're going to watch television?"

"We can't stay in bed all day."

"Why not?"

"Because people have to work." She picked up her notepad and looked at the pages of lyrics she'd written since she arrived in Aspen Cove. She had a whole album penned, from a song of hope called 'One Hundred Wishes' to a love song called 'In the Gray'.

"Speaking of work, all we need is a studio and a bass player to fill out your crew."

"Seriously? Dave has fired everyone else?" The thought of Dave Belton made Samantha's blood boil. She'd fantasized several times a day about seeing him face to face. Each time in her imagination, she fisted up and let him have it.

In reality, that wouldn't happen because the one thing Samantha knew about Dave was, he'd never let her win. She might get the first word in, maybe even get a hit, but he'd come out the victor.

"Yep, everyone but the bass player."

She set her soda can on the table and rolled up to a standing position. Samantha paced the room in front of the fireplace. "I haven't heard from him in days. I don't get what his end game is. If I don't have a crew, I can't make the music he wants. Where is this going?"

"You know him. He's killing you by a thousand tiny cuts. He doesn't know you've hired everyone. I've told them not to say anything. I'm pretty sure he thinks once your soft heart bleeds for a while, you'll give in. He knows you too well."

Deanna was right. She'd do anything for her crew. She'd sacrifice herself for them if she had to, but over the last two weeks, she realized she didn't have to. She held all the cards. She could move forward without Dave, but he'd never survive without her. She liked the power that position gave her.

"That was the old Samantha. That girl is gone, and in her place is me. I'll still bleed for my crew, but I can no longer fear Dave. It gives him too much power. Too much control."

"Rahrrr," Deanna growled. "Who let you out of your cage?"

"Me. I broke out. I'm tired of living in captivity. Tired of letting life live me instead of the other way around." A light knock sounded at the door. "Gotta go. Dalton's here."

"Skip *Supernatural* and go for the sheets," Deanna said before Samantha hung up. She had to agree. The sheets sounded appealing.

She rushed to the door. "You could have walked inside," she said as she swung it wide open, but it wasn't Dalton standing in front of her. It was Dave Belton, and he was pissed.

Her inner lion roared and then whimpered.

"You need to leave."

He flicked the stub of his filterless cigarette onto the deck and stepped forward.

She stepped back, her eyes on the hot ember and the wood.

"I don't need to do anything." He leaned against the rail of her back porch like he belonged there. "You need to do a lot. You can start by apologizing and packing."

She stepped forward and closed the door behind her. With the rubber sole of her tennis shoe, she ground the ash into the wood surface until it was extinguished. "You can burn down my house, but you won't get your way." All Dave thought about was Dave. It showed in every action from what he said to the careless tossing of his ember. "I'm not coming with you. You need to leave," she repeated. She hated the way her voice shook. What would Deanna think now that her roar had turned into a meow?

He shifted back and forth like a boxer. *Definitely high.* Dave always got jittery when he was coked out. "You need to come with me." He reached forward and gripped her left wrist, squeezing it hard.

"Don't touch me," she yelled. She pulled back, breaking his iron-fisted hold.

He raised his hands as if in surrender, but she knew better. Dave wasn't one to throw in the towel. "Look at you." He scanned her body from head to toe. "Two weeks, and you've gone to shit. You're fat and out of shape. Your hair ..." He shook his head. "It's a good thing I'm here. You've had your fun, now it's time to get back to work." He shriveled his nose in the way people did when they smelled something bad. "We have so much work to do."

"No." She had no idea where the word came from or where she got the strength to shout it. No one said no to Dave.

He pushed forward, taking a threatening step in her direction. "You owe me."

That statement was laughable. She pressed herself to the door. "I don't owe you anything. You've made a fortune on my talents. Without me, you have nothing." Gone was any semblance of calm. Her voice hit a decibel level that shook the windows behind her.

"I made you," he yelled.

"Wrong. *I* made *you*. No more. I don't need you to manage me. I'm a twenty-nine-year-old woman."

"Then act like it." He reached for her again and clamped his hand over her already sore wrist.

There was a flurry of motion. Several reporters stood by the lake, watching the action unfold. To Samantha's left, she watched Dalton come out of his cabin and take in the scene. A murderous look fell over his face when he saw Dave's hand on her. He hopped over the rail of his deck and raced forward. She knew in her heart if Dalton got to her before she took control of the situation, he'd be in jail for another murder.

Instead of allowing that to happen, Samantha pulled her right fist back and swung with all the might a hundred-and-ten-pound woman could throw. One hundred and ten because she knew she'd gained some weight. Her pants were tight, and the asshole told her she was fat. That was reason enough for her to strike. Add to that ten years of abuse, and she had her justification. When she connected with his nose, she heard the crunch of cartilage or bone.

Dave let her go. Both of his hands went to his face, where blood dripped between his fingers to her deck. He staggered back and stumbled down the stairs to the pine covered ground.

Dalton bolted past Dave and straight to Samantha, who cradled her right hand to her chest. She'd never hit anyone before. Inside, she felt amazing. She'd finally stuck up for herself. She'd shut a bully down. She didn't believe in fighting violence with violence, but with Dalton rushing to her aid, she had little choice but to get Dave's hands off of her before Dalton put his on the asshole.

"Are you okay?" Dalton placed himself between Samantha and Dave.

"You stupid bitch," Dave yelled from his place on the ground. "You've done it now." He stumbled to his feet and came forward. He was high, and high never meant smart.

Samantha tried to move in front of Dalton, but he kept her pinned behind him.

"You need to back away." Dalton's voice was low and deadly.

"Or what? Are you going to kill me too?" Dave pulled his phone out of his pocket.

"Dalton, stop. I'm hurt, and Dave Belton isn't worth it." She knew if she distracted him, he'd come to her rescue. It wasn't a lie. She was hurt. The crunch she heard was more than Dave's nose if the pain shooting through her hand was any hint. "I think I broke my hand."

By this time, the waterfront was full of paparazzi. They didn't care if they were breaking the law by trespassing on private property. All they cared about was getting the shot.

"I'm calling the police," Dave said.

Samantha peeked around Dalton's big body and said, "Good, you're going to need them when I press charges."

Her heart sank when she heard the asshole talk into his phone, "I want to press charges against Dalton Black. He assaulted me."

Samantha's world turned dark. "You liar. I hit you."

Dave hung up the phone. "Who will believe that? This only ends one way, Samantha. You come back to California, and it'll all go away. Stay here, and I'll make sure everything you have goes up in flames."

Minutes later, Sheriff Cooper arrived. He took statements from everyone, then turned to Dalton. "Dave Belton accused you of hitting him."

Dalton looked at Samantha and back to Sheriff Cooper. "He's a liar."

"I'm taking you both in until this is all cleared up," the sheriff said.

A gut-wrenching cry left Samantha. "He didn't do it." She raced toward Dalton, throwing her arms around him. Ignoring the pain in her hand because it came nowhere close to the pain in her heart. "I'm so sorry. This is my fault. I'll fix it."

Dalton cupped her face and kissed her. "No, sweetheart." He looked at the idiot. "This is his fault."

While Sheriff Cooper placed Dalton in his cruiser, Deputy Sheriff Bancroft took custody of Dave. It was a bittersweet moment to see him being placed in the police car. A heartbreaking moment to watch Dalton being driven away.

Standing alone on the back porch of her cabin, she turned to the press. "You wanted a story?" she yelled. "This is your story. Will you tell the truth? I challenge you to report the damn truth for a change."

Cannon came running up the beach. "What the hell happened?"

Samantha broke down and cried. "I've ruined Dalton's life."

Cannon hung his arm over her shoulders and walked her to his truck. "Let's get you to Doc's, then we'll figure out what the hell we're going to do about Dalton."

Samantha explained the situation to Cannon on their way into town. "He didn't do anything. He raced to help me. I'm the one who hit Dave."

"Any witnesses?"

"Yes, many. But will they come forward?" Samantha wasn't sure. It was his word against hers. Dave Belton's accusation turned everything upside down.

CHAPTER TWENTY-FIVE

Sitting in a jail cell wasn't the worst thing. Sitting in a jail cell and knowing Samantha was hurt and alone was insufferable. Having Dave Belton in the cell next to him was like throwing salt on an open wound.

"She'll be gone by the time you get out of here. That's her MO. She grew up running from trouble," Dave taunted Dalton from his cell.

It was a good thing he couldn't see him or get to him. All he wanted right now was to shut the asshole up. "You don't know what you're talking about."

"Ten years. I've had her for ten years. She's almost like a daughter."

Dalton sat on the cement bench and leaned against the wall. "That's irony for you. Her father was an abusive asshole too. If she wasn't contractually bound, you'd already be in her rearview mirror."

"Unlike you, she'll never leave me. I hold all the cards. You may have your dick inside of her, but my influence is wrapped around her so tightly, she can't breathe unless I say so. She's weak and scared. Always has been. Always will be."

"How's that nose?" Dalton hated that Samantha hurt her hand, but loved that she stood her ground and defended herself. "Scratch that. How does it feel to know someone you consider weak and scared kicked your ass?"

"Probably better than knowing you're going back to jail because they think you did it."

Dalton laughed. "You have no idea who you're dealing with. If I had been the one to hit you, you wouldn't have gotten up. They don't call my right hand the fist of death for nothing." It wasn't something he liked to brag about, but Dave Belton needed to know he got off easy. If Dalton had made it to Samantha before she threw that punch, Dave would be in the hospital or the morgue instead of jail.

"I'd gladly do time for Samantha. I can understand your need to lie. I mean, she's a hundred pounds soaking wet. Not sure my ego could take that beating either. I get why you have to invent a story. Tall tales compensate for your little wiener."

"You're lucky there's a wall separating us."

"Trembling over here." Dalton shook with a silent chuckle. The problem with guys like Dave was they were all talk and no action. They hid behind words and women. "Too bad I can still hear you. Makes me want to give you that smack down you're telling everyone about. Do you need a doctor? There's one across the street. He'll even give you a Life Saver if you don't cry."

"You two done?" Sheriff Cooper walked around the corner with keys jingling in his hands.

Dalton heard Dave shuffle and walk to the bars. "It's about time you came to let me out."

"About that." Sheriff Cooper stood between the two cells so both men could see him. "Seems to be a discrepancy with your story."

"Is this some small town, favoritism bullshit going on?" Dalton couldn't see Dave's face, but he could hear the rage in his voice. "I'll sue the hell out of you and this town if you don't let me go right now."

"There's a problem. I thought maybe you'd like to tell me what happened one more time."

Sheriff Cooper looked at Dalton. He wasn't exactly wearing a smile on his face, more of a pay-attention expression that Dalton found interesting.

"I told you already. I was talking to Indigo ... I mean Samantha, and out of nowhere Dalton Black attacked me."

"From which direction did he approach?" Sheriff Cooper jotted some things in his notepad as Dave recited his lie.

"He's so big, he was everywhere at once."

"Did you try to defend yourself?"

"I didn't have time. He punched me, and I fell down the stairs."

"Hmm." The sheriff walked towards Dalton's cell and unlocked the door. "You're free to go."

He exited and stood in front of Dave's cell. The man had his red face pressed to the bars. "You've got to be kidding me? He's a felon."

Sheriff shook his head. "Ex-felon. He did his time."

"He hit me."

"Deputy Bancroft? Please bring the evidence back here."

Seconds later, Mark Bancroft walked back, carrying an expensive looking camera. "Hold this button." The sheriff called Dalton over, and they stood in front of Dave's cell. He was far enough away that Dave couldn't touch anything or anyone, but he had a great view of the entire event captured pixel by pixel. The sheriff held the button down and displayed the pictures in rapid succession like a video.

"Seems to me that you assaulted Ms. White and she defended herself. She's across the street getting a cast put on, and may press charges. You have the right to do likewise, but the evidence is pretty damning. Would you like to call your lawyer?"

Dalton didn't wait to hear Dave's answer. He bolted from the back room and raced across the street to Doc Parker's clinic.

Doc was putting the last layer of plaster in place when he walked inside. As he did for every patient, he unwrapped a cherry Life Saver and popped it into Samantha's mouth when she opened it to say something.

"Mmm," she moaned. "That's almost worth breaking my hand."

Doc turned to Dalton. "Might as well look at you while you're here. Take off your pants."

Dalton stared at the Doc and then at Samantha. "Now?"

"Don't be shy. I'm sure she's seen it all already."

Samantha laughed and waggled her perfectly plucked brows. "Yeah, Dalton, take off your pants."

"In a second." He walked to her and cradled her newly cast hand in his. "Does it hurt?"

She shook her head. "Less now than it did when it was pressed against Dave's nose."

Doc walked to the door. "I'll get her some pain meds. When I get back, only one of you better be naked."

He shut the door behind him, giving them some privacy.

"Answer me truthfully. Are you in pain?"

She lifted the black cast. Her choice of color wasn't lost on him. "It's not that bad. Doc says it's a hairline fracture. Should heal fine."

He cupped her face. "You were a badass."

She smiled and sat taller. "I kind of was. I feel good about it all." She lifted her good hand and pulled him down for a kiss. "I'm glad Jake got those pictures."

"You know him?"

"Yes, he's around a lot. I told him I'd give him an exclusive interview a few days ago. I guess that went a long way in his book. He chased me down here and showed me the footage he recorded. I sent him straight to the sheriff's office."

"Dave is furious."

Her smile lit up the room. "Dave is fired. I put in a call to my agent, and he's agreed to end the contract. I was so stupid to sign such a long deal with both of them. Talk about young and dumb. I didn't know any better."

"That's the thing: When you know better, you do better."

She narrowed her eyes at him. "Oprah said that a long time ago."

He'd never admit his love for Oprah to anyone but her. "Her

show was my guilty pleasure for six years. It was all reruns because she went off the air in 2011, but I watched and learned."

She pressed her lips to his. "You are always a surprise to me."

"One of you better be undressed, and it better be Dalton," Doc's voice sounded from the end of the hallway.

"That's my cue." He unbuttoned his jeans and let them fall to the floor.

She hopped off the table to get a good look at his leg. "It still looks so painful."

"You have the most amazing way of making me forget the discomfort."

Samantha hummed, which made it near impossible for Dalton to not get hard. Her voice did things to his heart, but when she hummed in that low throaty way, it vibrated through his body and settled between his legs.

"You ready?"

Dalton hopped onto the cold table and eyed Samantha. "Behave yourself."

"What? I'm working on a melody." She went back to humming the low tones that made him stiff. He kept his eyes on Doc's bulbous nose and overgrown eyebrows. That worked well to kill his desire.

Doc gave him a quick once-over and applied some antibiotic ointment to the deepest wounds. "You'll live." He walked to the door. "I don't normally tell my patients to spend more time inside, but I'm thinking you two are dangerous when left in the wild. Go home and climb into bed."

Dalton's eyes grew wide. "You heard him, he said we have to get into bed."

Samantha tossed him his jeans. "I heard him. Hurry up."

Dalton caught Doc before he walked out the door. "No Life Saver for me?"

Doc nodded toward Samantha. "She got the last one. You'll have to see if she'll share."

Samantha bolted past Doc toward the pharmacy. "Not sharing. You'll have to get your own."

"Kids," Doc grumbled.

Because they'd both been driven to town, they walked back home. Dalton wrapped his arm around Samantha's shoulders. He couldn't help hearing Dave's words in his head. "She'll be gone by the time you get out of here."

"I know your instinct to leave is strong … but don't."

She slowed her walk to a crawl. "Tell me something good that's happened since my arrival?"

It twisted his gut that she didn't see them as being something good. "*We're* good. Don't forget, we're stronger together."

She held up her cast. "I don't know. I'm pretty strong on my own." She threaded her left arm through his right and leaned against him. "I'm pretty sure Aspen Cove will breathe a sigh of relief when I'm gone."

"If you leave, I may never breathe again." Dalton hated that he'd let her get so deeply imbedded inside his heart. Weeks ago, he teased his friends about catching a love virus. Apparently, he had been exposed and had no immunity to Samantha White. He was head-over-heels in love with her, and that scared him more than anything.

CHAPTER TWENTY-SIX

They'd almost made it to her cabin when the sheriff pulled his cruiser beside them.

He rolled down his window. "You didn't stop by to fill out the paperwork to press charges."

Samantha bit her lip. "Sorry." She had glanced at the sheriff's office when they walked through town. She'd taken care of the Dave problem when she called the Shepherd Agency. To do anything more would be like poking a bear with a sharp stick.

"I can't hold him without charges." Sheriff Cooper exited the cruiser and stood against the door. A few bees flew by to investigate and then left.

Samantha looked past the boxed hives to where a few reporters covered in netting held their cameras at the ready. She'd always hated how the press invaded her privacy, but her thoughts on that changed the minute Jake offered pictures to exonerate Dalton.

"I'm not sure that's wise."

Dalton stepped in front of her. "Press charges, or he'll come back for round two like Todd."

She knew they were looking out for her, but that was part of the problem. No one hesitated to tell her what they wanted her to do. No one asked her what she wanted, and right now that was peace and time alone with Dalton.

"I don't have to press charges, and I don't want to." She hated that she sounded so snippy, but pressing charges kept Dave in her life. She wanted him gone. She looked at Dalton. "It's the week of second chances. Todd got one. You got one. Dave gets one."

"So, no charges?" Sheriff Cooper frowned.

"Not unless he's charging me."

"Nope."

Samantha shrugged. "No charges, then."

"Can't say I'm on the same page as you. He seems like an unpredictable man."

Understatement. "I want this to be over. Charging him keeps him in my life."

"Your call." He opened the door and climbed back into his cruiser. "I'll take him to his car and escort him to the town line. Keep your eyes open." He rolled up his window and headed back toward town.

"It's a mistake to let him off. He broke your hand." Dalton glanced down at the black cast.

"I broke my hand on his nose. Really, he could press charges. He's not. Let it go." She walked past him, taking a circuitous route around the buzzing hives toward the remaining reporters. She had to give Abby Garrett credit. Everyone was afraid of bees.

She looked behind her and waved for Dalton to follow. He looked at the hives and frowned. Even Mr. Big and Brawny feared the buzz.

She approached Jake and gave him a hug. "Thanks for coming to our rescue."

Dalton advanced with caution. She knew his experience with the press had been less than favorable. Hers had too, but maybe it was the way she thought of the press. She'd done a lot of swatting at them and avoiding them. Like the bees, they stung when they weren't happy.

"Dalton? Do you have time for a few questions?"

The grimace on his face screamed no, but he walked forward and stood next to Samantha. His body was tense until she leaned into him and rested her head on his chest.

"Can we get a shot of you two?" Jake asked. He didn't have his camera pointed and focused like the others. He held it up and lifted his shoulders in question.

She turned to Dalton. "You okay with that?"

"Sure." He wrapped his arm around her. She settled her cast against his stomach. "Anyone have a Sharpie that would show up on black?"

A young photographer in the back held up a pack of metallic, felt-tip pens. "These should work, they're good for proofs."

Dalton took out the silver Sharpie and drew a heart on Samantha's cast. In the center he wrote, "It's all about love."

Ray asked how they'd met, and Dalton told him that Samantha almost burned down her cabin the first night she was here.

"Cooking?" he asked.

"No, trying not to freeze," she replied.

"Do you love her?" Jake asked Dalton.

He looked at her and didn't deny it. "How could I not? Look at her." He smiled. "And have you heard her sing?"

"What about you, Indigo?" a girl off to the side called. "Are you in love with Dalton Black?" Samantha waited for her to say *convicted killer* as if it were his last name, but she didn't.

Samantha looked into Dalton's eyes. She'd never said the words to him. She wanted it to be a private moment, but to say anything less than the truth would be wrong.

"How could I not be? Look at him." She squeezed her arms around his waist. "Have you tasted anything he cooks?" She implied that love was there, but the words were for him alone.

There was collective conversation about the diner and his blue-plate specials. Turns out they had put two and two together, but as long as he was cooking, they didn't care.

Ray stepped forward. "What's next for you?"

She honestly couldn't say. "I was supposed to do a benefit concert for women and children suffering from domestic violence, but the misrepresentation of Dalton in the press has put that in jeopardy."

"It has?" Dalton stepped away. "They canceled the concert because of me?" He ran his hand through his hair. "That's ridiculous. Those families need support." He paced in front of the hives. It was said that animals and insects could sense tension and fear. The hive buzzed louder. Samantha and the press moved farther away. "It's never going to end, is it? I did something six years ago, and it changed my life. I did my time. When will it go away? Hundreds of abused women and children will suffer because I protected Bethany Waters. It hardly seems fair. And you know what?" He turned toward the small gathering. "I'd do it again." Dalton turned and walked toward his cabin.

Samantha stood in the center of the group. She pointed toward Dalton's retreating figure. "That right there is your story. *He's* not a monster. He *killed* a monster. He knew exactly what that looked like growing up. He was the son of one. I knew what that looked like too. When I was nine, my mother and I went on the run. We looked over our shoulders until I was sixteen. That's when we found out he'd died in a single-car accident. The scariest thing about that day was, he died in the town where we lived. He'd found us and had gone to a bar to celebrate."

"Did he say Bethany Waters?" Jake asked as he jotted down the name.

"Yes. It's public record. His entire story is public record if anyone wanted to know the truth. The problem is, the truth doesn't always sell the story." She handed the silver pen back to its owner and looked down at her cast. *"It's all about love."* That was a wise thing to remember.

Samantha found Dalton at his place. He was in the kitchen doing what he did best. "Hey." He continued to season the roast he had on the counter. "Look at me." She stepped in front of him and pressed her head to his chest. "It's all right."

"No, it's not. Look at what my presence has done to you—to others."

She sighed. Not the sigh of surrender, but a sigh of heartwarming goodness. "Yes, look what you did to me. You cared for me. You protected me. You loved me. Despite everything that's happened over the last couple of weeks, I'd do it all over again because I'm a better person when I'm with you."

"It's a good thing Dave never let you out of his sight, or you might know what a good man looks like, and I'd never have had a chance with you."

"Don't bring up Dave when I'm feeling all warm and fuzzy and romantic."

He pulled a bag of baby carrots out of the refrigerator and spread them around the roast. "Is your agent really going to let him go?" Next came the new potatoes.

"Dalton, you're shriveling my libido with talk about work." She plucked a stray carrot from the bag. "That's what he said. He told me he put in a call and will wait until Dave calls back."

"You think he'll do it?" He turned and slid the pan into the preheated oven.

"If he wants to work with me, he'll follow through. My contract is up after the next album and the benefit concert."

She reached around him for a glass, filled it with water, and popped two of the pain pills Doc Parker gave her. "Do you want to talk about Dave and Oliver, or do you want to take my mind off how much my hand hurts? I'll take your mind off how unfair the world can be."

He set the timer. "We have a couple of hours. Let's go to bed."

"Now, that's the best thing I've heard all day."

CHAPTER TWENTY-SEVEN

There was nothing more comforting than comfort food. Pot roast with carrots and potatoes topped that list with honors. They sat in front of his big screen television, ate, and binged *Supernatural* like it was crack and they were addicts.

A fire crackled in the fireplace. Samantha curled into Dalton's side. It was hard to think this wasn't ideal, but their relationship was complicated. In bed, they were perfection. In the bubble of their world, they were ideal, but they hadn't talked about tomorrow or next week or next year.

"This is perfect," he said. He moved them both so they were lying on the couch with her back to his front.

"It's too bad it isn't real." She melted against him like her body no longer had bones.

They'd loved the tension out of each other for an hour earlier, and she put tension back in him with those words.

"What part isn't real?"

She turned around to face him. "The part we don't talk about. The part where I have to go back to my life and leave you to yours."

"We can work it out." He had to stay positive, or the feelings of loss could swallow him whole. The thought of a day without Samantha would be as bad as the day the door closed and locked him in prison. That might have been better because he had a definitive date when things would go back to normal—his new normal.

Samantha lived states away. She spent months on the road. Her lifestyle didn't lend itself to normal. He remembered Doc's words. Samantha didn't come here to be Indigo. She came here to figure out who she was.

"You want a long-distance relationship?"

He rose up on one elbow and pushed the hair that had fallen into her face behind her ear so he could see her eyes. All truth was in Samantha's dark eyes. Looking into hers, he saw that she loved him as much as he loved her.

"Love looks different for everyone." He kissed her forehead. "I thought my life was pretty good before you came along. You showed up, and *bam*—I realized I was lying to myself. I'd be lying to you if I said long distance is what I want. It's not. I want you in my life and my bed every night, but I'll take what I can get. Some of you is infinitely better than none of you."

"You really should set your standards higher." She snuggled into his side and inhaled. She breathed him in like she was collecting his scent for a future he wouldn't be in.

"Higher than a hot-as-hell pop star who rocks my world and makes me feel like I can conquer anything when she's near?"

She laughed, and the vibration felt good against his chest. "When you put it that way, I guess I'm quite a catch."

"Have I caught you?"

"Dalton Black, I fell for you the day you left flowers and milk on my porch."

"Don't forget the bread and eggs," he said. "I only bring eggs to girls I'm sure to fall in love with." He pulled her against him and held her tight.

Her muffled voice asked, "Are there a lot of girls you've loved?"

"Three in my whole life."

She narrowed her eyes. He loved the way she couldn't help her jealousy.

"Were they pretty?"

"Stunning."

"Hmm. Do you see them around?"

He thumbed her chin so she was forced to look at him. "One is my mother. I see her regularly. One was Bea. It was a sad day when she left us, but she left a legacy of love. The last girl ... lately I've seen her a lot, but who knows what the future holds. All I know is I want one with her. I love you, Samantha. I don't care that you're a pop star. I don't care if you have a hundred houses dotted around the world or a million dollars in the bank. None of that matters to me. All I care about is making you happy and making you fall in love with me."

She swallowed hard like she was eating sand. "I've never said these words to anyone, but I love you, Dalton. Not because you're sex on a stick or because you have the most talented tongue in the universe or because you cook better than Bobby Flay. All I want is to care for you and love you so you don't regret the day you left me flowers and milk and bread and eggs."

She kissed him tenderly and passionately, and although she said the words for the first time, his heart felt like she'd told him a thousand times. When the kiss ended, he rose to a seated position. "Bobby Flay has cooked for you?"

She shook from a full belly laugh. "Yes. So have Wolfgang Puck, Gordon Ramsay, and Mario Batali, but they've got nothing on you." She curled into the corner of his leather couch and propped her feet on his lap. "You think I have a hundred houses?"

"No, but it sounded good. I imagine if we're going to try to make a go of this thing, and since we both let the L-word out, we should be transparent about our lives."

"You want transparency?"

"No, all I want is to be honest with you. Our relationship started on a mound of omissions. I'm an ex-felon. I killed a man. I'm a cook. Actually, I'm a cook at a diner. My employment potential is limited.

I'll never be able to give you what you're used to, but I'll love you deeply. I don't care if your hair is blue, brown, or gray. I'll love you anyway." He reached over and laid his hand on her heart. "I love you here, and that's all that matters."

She pressed her left hand over his and pinned it to her chest.

"I'm a pop star. I love the music, but hate the fame. I have brown hair and plan to keep it that way. I own two properties. One is a house outside Los Angeles. One is a tiny cabin in Aspen Cove. I prefer Aspen Cove. I have a million dollars. Not on me but invested or in the bank. In fact, I have several, but it doesn't have the value that your love does. I don't know where all this will lead, but I'd like to find out."

She crawled across his body and straddled his lap. What they didn't finish on the couch, they completed in the bedroom. Exhausted, Samantha fell asleep naked in his arms. He wondered how he'd gotten so lucky. It was funny how luck came packaged as trouble. Samantha was that, but she was so much more.

He'd dozed off when the acrid smell of smoke filled the air. He was certain he'd banked the fire. His confidence faltered when the fire alarm rang through the silence.

He jumped out of his bed and into his jeans. He tugged on his boots and shook Samantha awake.

"Sweetheart, you need to get up. Get dressed."

She groaned and buried her head under the pillow.

"Samantha," he roared. "Get up. There's a fire."

That was one word that could wake anyone from a deep sleep. She stumbled out of bed and struggled to get her clothes on. Dalton ran through his house but saw nothing. The fire alarms wailed in the distance.

When he stepped onto his porch, he saw Samantha's cabin engulfed in flames. He called it in. They had a phone tree for the volunteer firefighters, which included every able-bodied man in Aspen Cove.

Minutes later, while the wood of her cabin crackled and splintered under the heat, dozens of men donned whatever protective gear they had and went to work dousing the flames. Sage and Katie ran to get to Samantha, while Cannon and Bowie jumped into the melee. Even Doc Parker was there, beating back the fire so it didn't spread. In minutes, Samantha's car was set ablaze. As Bobby Williams raced with the hose to douse the new flames, it exploded, sending him back a dozen feet.

Dalton wanted to race to his friend, but Doc was already headed in that direction. The flames were out of control in the house. If they didn't get them under control, everyone nearby would lose their homes, including him.

The fire was already licking at the siding of his cabin. The freshly sandblasted section didn't stand a chance. Phillip Butler showed up with a case of bottled water from his Corner Store, and his wife carried boxes of snacks. It was a welcome gift for the firefighters.

The Dawson's only son and Lawyer Frank Arden showed up minutes later. They took charge of a hose and kept a steady stream of water where Dalton's siding had turned black.

He looked around for Samantha. He found her standing near Bowie and Katie's cabin with a look of horror on her face. He followed her line of sight to where Bobby laid on the ground with flames licking at his already burned skin. Dalton raced toward his friend to get him as far away from the smoke and flames as possible.

CHAPTER TWENTY-EIGHT

Samantha screamed. The scene was pure chaos as Doc rushed forward to provide care to Bobby, who only moments ago was on fire. Were it not for his quick actions, he would now be engulfed in flames.

Bowie rushed over and told Katie to pack up Sahara and go to Ben and Maisey's. Sage went straight into nurse mode. Samantha stood out of the way and knew this was all her fault. Dave Belton's words would haunt her for the rest of her life. *"Stay here, and I'll make sure everything you have goes up in flames."*

Doc asked Sage to call for an ambulance. He stood up and looked through the fog of black smoke. His hand went to his chest, and he hit the floor like a felled tree. Samantha raced over to help. She and Sage pulled Doc across the street. When he came to, he wasn't the same cantankerous old man she knew him to be. He was pale and quiet, and his breath wheezed from his chest.

Dalton carried Bobby Williams across the street and laid him down. "Call Louise and tell her he's hurt."

"I'll be okay," Bobby said. "Louise needs to be with the kids. I don't want her anywhere near this." Samantha recognized the man as the guy in the diner with the pregnant wife and seven children. Her heart broke. Holes burned through his jeans to show blistering and charred skin.

A loud crash drew their attention. The roof of Samantha's cabin gave way, collapsing into the house. Hot embers floated through the air.

"Go to my place and get as much ice and cold water as you can. There are baggies in the pantry. We need to stop the heat," Sage said.

Samantha took off like a sprinter toward the bed and breakfast. Because Sage often had guests, she was stocked with bags of ice. Samantha made quick work of gathering supplies and carried half her body weight in ice back to Sage.

"Get Doc to drink some water." Sage filled bags with ice and water and laid the cold packs on Bobby's legs.

Five minutes later, a hysterical Louise arrived. She dropped to her knees in front of her husband. "Don't you leave me, Bobby Williams. I can't raise eight kids by myself."

He raised a burned hand to her cheek. "Louise, I'm not going anywhere. We still have babies to make." The shrill of the sirens broke through the noise of the fire. Who would have thought a blaze could be so loud? It was almost deafening.

When the paramedics arrived, they praised Sage for her quick thinking by placing the ice packs on Bobby's burns and keeping Doc calm and quiet. He had a reputation for being a fighter, so to see him in such a sorry state shocked everyone.

Forty minutes later, two fire engines from Copper Creek came to put out what the volunteer force couldn't with their limited equipment.

Samantha couldn't believe that the town of Aspen Cove didn't have its own fire department. Then again, Aspen Cove didn't have much.

The sun was rising when the last of the volunteers left. Cannon opened the bar for drinks, and Dalton told everyone he'd cook them breakfast if they gave him an hour.

Samantha sat across the street and looked at the utter devastation. Even Abby's bees had suffered. The ones that couldn't escape were devoured by the flames.

Her cabin had been reduced to a pile of smoke and ashes. Dalton's place stood, but the charred siding was sooty and black.

Sheriff Cooper took off, lights flashing and sirens wailing. She overheard Mark Bancroft tell everyone the arson case in Copper Creek had been solved. Turns out it wasn't arson after all. The house around the lake had burned down because of faulty wiring. Only Samantha's house was burned to the ground on purpose.

Dave Belton was caught racing out of town with enough accelerant to burn down the state of Colorado. He was always a man of his word. He'd made sure that she had only one option left, and that was to leave.

"Sweetheart?"

"I'm okay." She looked at what was left of her cabin. Among the ashes stood the fireplace. How funny that Dalton had accused her of trying to burn down the house, and it burned down anyway. ·

"I'm sure your insurance will rebuild the cabin. It will be better than before." Dalton squatted in front of her. His face was covered in soot and grime, but he was as sexy as ever. "It will turn out okay. It's all over."

He was right. It was over, but it would never be okay. She had to leave before another person suffered because of her. The problem was, Dalton would never let her go. He didn't blame her, despite the news of Dave's setting the fire spreading faster than the flames themselves. She blamed herself.

"This is all my fault."

"No. It's not. You didn't light the match, he did."

"I lit the match by pissing him off. I turned an ember into a blaze. You were right, I should have pressed charges. Had I done that, Bobby and Doc wouldn't be hurt. Bobby has seven kids and one on the way. I could have orphaned them all." Tears raced down her cheeks.

Dalton pulled her to standing and wrapped his strong arms around her. He smelled so good, like pine trees and pure man.

"Bobby will be fine. His burns will heal. Louise will take care of him. Doc has smoke inhalation. Some burning in his lungs. He's too ornery to stay down long. I'm worried about you. You look exhausted. Let's get you home and to bed."

She breathed him in, trying to save the smell and feel of him into her memory. There was only one thing left to do, and that was to leave. She'd make sure Aspen Cove and its people were cared for. When she first arrived, Katie told her that Aspen Cove took care of its own. Part of taking care of the ones you loved was protecting them. She was a liability.

Dave would no longer be a threat, but what about the next crazy person like Todd, or an overzealous paparazzo who would do anything to get the next sale-worthy photo? She couldn't risk it. She couldn't risk them.

"I am tired." Exhausted didn't begin to describe how she felt. She was devastated and hollowed out. Conflicted about what she wanted and what was best. Her heart told her to go to the diner and help Dalton serve the men who helped save the neighborhood. Without them, Samantha's house wouldn't have been the only one to burn. It would have spread down the line to Dalton's, Katie's, and Sage's. She owed them. Her payment would be her absence. She'd set up a fund to pay for Bobby's and Doc's medical bills. She'd make sure the town had the equipment they needed even if she had to build a firehouse. She'd ensure any lost wages were replaced. It was the least she could do. It was the easy thing to do. The hardest thing would be kissing Dalton goodbye and knowing it was for forever.

While Dalton took a shower, she gathered the few belongings she had and raced to the bed when she heard the shower turn off. Dalton appeared with droplets of water running down his chest and a towel tied around his waist. All she wanted to do was pull him into bed and ask him to hold her, but that would make it harder to leave, so she closed her eyes when he entered the room and pretended she was asleep. After he dressed, he kissed her and said, "I love you."

She fought the urge to respond. The minute the front door closed, she jumped from the bed, called a car service in Copper Creek, and arranged for transportation.

An hour later, Samantha slipped out of Dalton's cabin and into a black town car. She made a quick stop at the bakery to tack her wishes onto the board. Only one was for her, the rest were for those she cared about.

She wished for Doc's quick recovery.

That Bobby Williams would be home soon with his family.

For Sage and Cannon to have the perfect wedding.

That Katie would have the boy she dreamed of having.

For Lydia to find a job.

That Cannon and Bowie would be there for Dalton.

And that Dalton would forgive her for everything.

Finally, it looked like luck was on her side because only Ben was present when she tacked the notes to the board. She bought a muffin for her driver. It was Thursday, and the poppy seed muffins couldn't be ignored. When she climbed into the back of the car, she curled into a tight ball and cried for the entire three-hour drive to Denver.

CHAPTER TWENTY-NINE

Dalton's ass was dragging when he entered the cabin. All he wanted to do was crawl into bed next to Samantha and hold her in his arms.

Though during the fire he appeared to be in control the whole time, he hadn't been. That asshole Dave could have killed them both. If they'd been in her cabin, who knows what could have happened? The dried wood and log siding burned like a grassfire. It went up so fast, there might not have been time to escape. It twisted his insides to see how close he came to losing his newfound love and happiness.

Samantha felt responsible, but she wasn't. Not once during breakfast did anyone say anything negative about her. They talked about the age of the house. That no one knew she was famous. That went a long way in her favor because weren't they all just people? Mostly the townsfolk talked about the idiot who thought bullying her could drive her away.

He toed off his boots at the door and took a deep breath. The air smelled like her under the lingering scent of smoke and fire. She was flowers and happiness and sunshine. He hurried down the hallway, and turned into the bedroom, only to find it dark, gloomy and empty.

He knew right away that she'd left him. Dave had won. There

wasn't a trace of her around. Her phone was gone. She always tossed her bag and shoes in the corner, but the space was vacant. The only thing that remained was a note left on his pillow.

Dalton,

These are the hardest words I'll ever write. How do I tell the person I'm in love with goodbye? It would be impossible unless I knew that leaving was the right thing to do. I'm so sorry that I brought so much hurt to you and Aspen Cove. I will always love this town and the people who made it feel like home. I will always love you.

No matter where our lives lead us, please know that your name will be tattooed on my heart forever.

I am Samantha White.

You are Dalton Black.

The beauty of us will always lie in the gray.

Love

Samantha

Watermarks from her fallen tears marred the paper.

"She free-birded me and never intends to come back." He crumbled the page and tossed it across the room. "That's bullshit, and it's not going to happen."

Dalton started a pot of coffee. Outside of her new cell number, he had no way of contacting her. No way of knowing where she'd gone.

He dialed her number and was crushed when it went directly to voicemail.

A WEEK LATER, he was still reaching out to her fan site. Sending letters to her record label and leaving messages with her assistant. He followed her on social media. Bought every one of her albums. Listening to her sing brought both joy and sorrow. He loved and hated the videos he found online where she talked to her fans about never giving up and finding your purpose.

He wanted to call her a liar. She'd given up on them. Then again, she'd sacrificed her own happiness out of some misplaced need to protect him.

When the demolition company arrived to remove the debris, Dalton felt a glimmer of hope. Maybe she would rebuild her cabin and return to rebuild their relationship. That dream was dashed when the following week, a for sale sign went up on the land.

He sat in front of the Wishing Wall one day, eating carrot cake muffins. Katie came out of the back with a stack of notes in her hand. Every few weeks, she'd sit down at a table and grant wishes.

"You need anything?"

"Yes. I need Samantha to come back to me."

She tossed a baggie of notes on the table and went to get a cup of decaf coffee. It was always decaf. She joked about Bowie being the only stimulation her heart needed.

"You love her?"

"Yes. Isn't it obvious?"

She sat down and placed the wishes into piles. He knew the routine. Had seen it many times. Knew that she put them into piles of yes, no, and maybe. This time, she had a fourth pile.

"Why are you here? If you love her that much, go and get her."

"Like that's so easy. I don't even know where she is. She won't answer my calls. I've sent dozens of flowers to every Samantha White I can find in the Greater Los Angeles Area. I've got quite a fan club of my own now."

Katie laughed. "You know where she'll be next week."

He knew. She'd be at the concert to benefit victims of domestic violence. "I'm glad they didn't cancel the concert." Maybe her leaving him was good after all. At least the venue would be full and the money would go to a good cause.

She slid a pile of sticky notes to him. "I think these fall in your lane."

Dalton raised his brow in confusion. "I'm not the wish granter."

"Today you are, and if you decide you want to go after what's important, I can help. I used to be a Middleton, and that still holds some influence."

Dalton leaned back in his seat. The metal design cut into his back. He opened the first note in the pile. It was dated the day after Samantha arrived. *A kiss from Dalton Black would be nice.* In his mind, he said, *Granted.* The second note written in her precise tiny handwriting said, *Is it silly to wish for love?*

"No."

Katie looked up from her pile. "Excuse me?"

Dalton shook his head. "Nothing, I was thinking out loud."

She sipped her coffee. "Then say, yes."

"But it's not silly for her to wish for love."

"No, but it's silly for her to think she doesn't deserve it."

He agreed, but how could he convince her that she was worthy if he couldn't get in the same time zone as her?

He opened the other notes that had wishes from the press leaving him alone to her wish for him to forgive her.

He pulled out his phone and dialed his parole officer.

"You better not be in jail," she said. He could hear the whinny of a horse in the background.

"Hell, no." Thankfully, there was no paper trail of him getting detained weeks ago. If Lucy thought he'd been in trouble, she'd never allow him to leave the state. "I'm leaving the state for a short period. Thought I'd check in."

"You asking permission?"

Was he? The truth was, no. He'd be leaving whether or not she said it was okay.

"I'm not asking for your permission. I'm following your advice. I fell in love, and I'm making sure she knows it. She can run and hide, but I'll find her, and I'll bring her back. We've got memories and babies to make."

"Hmm, I didn't hear you right. Sounded like you were going to stalk and kidnap someone, but what I think you really meant was, you were going to travel somewhere to tell your woman you love her. That's what I heard, right?"

He laughed. "Yes, that's what I said."

She cleared her throat but still sounded like she'd smoked a pack that day. "Call me when you get back."

"Will do." Dalton ended the call and picked up the notes. He opened his wallet and slid them inside. "Now all I need is a way into the concert and a ticket to California."

Katie held up a finger. She dialed her phone. "Daddy, this is Katie. I need a favor."

Turns out that once a Middleton meant always a Middleton. And being a Middleton came with perks.

CHAPTER THIRTY

"Call him." Deanna flopped onto the sofa across from Samantha.

They sat in her Malibu Canyon house and looked out the wall of glass. The sky was blue and crystal clear, but her mood was black. Not even chocolate made her smile. What seemed like a reasonable choice a few weeks ago was clouded with uncertainty now.

She'd done what she could for Aspen Cove and followed up on the recovery of Doc and Bobby. She'd even taken measures to build the town a firehouse so they could have their own truck. If they couldn't afford to pay for firemen, she was prepared to cover that expense as well. No person should have to depend on volunteers to save their life.

Samantha thought she'd done the right thing by leaving, but her broken heart told her differently. She ached for Dalton. There wasn't a second of any day where she didn't think of him, feel the ghost of his love hold her, kiss her, and love her.

"I can't call him. I left him. He probably hates me." She'd recited the letter she'd written him over and over in her mind. "I'm a coward."

"Why do you keep saying that?"

"Because I couldn't face him. I left him a Dear John letter. Who does that? I write lyrics that every woman feels, but I couldn't talk to the man I love. I should have told him face to face, but I knew ... I knew he'd tell me to stay, and I knew I wouldn't say no."

"You need to fix this." Deanna kicked her feet up on the coffee table.

"I have. Everyone is okay. Workers will start on Dalton's house next week. He'll show up, and it will be done. I've set up funds for the injured. Planned for the future. It's fixed."

"For being such a smart woman, you are so stupid." Deanna turned her laptop toward Samantha. "Do you see this folder?" She pressed her computer across the space between them. "Over a hundred messages asking for you to call him. You think he wants to tell you he hates you? This *isn't* fixed."

"What was I supposed to do?" Her voice wavered. She thought she'd cried herself dry, but there seemed to be an endless supply of tears for Dalton.

"You were supposed to stay. You didn't, so the next best thing is to go home and make it right."

Samantha covered her face with her hands. "I don't have a home."

Deanna moved to the space beside her. "Home isn't always a place. It can be a feeling. It can be as simple as knowing someone loves you, no matter what." She pressed her finger against the computer screen. "Dalton Black is your home."

THREE DAYS LATER, Samantha stood backstage while the crowd chanted, "In-di-go, In-di-go, In-di-go". She couldn't believe that not too long ago a different crowd chanted the same. That night she'd walked into the mass of fans and disappeared, hoping to find clarity, only to come back more confused.

She adjusted the blue wig and applied her watermelon lip gloss.

It reminded her of Dalton. Everything reminded her of Dalton. Since her return, all she ate was grilled cheese and tomato soup because it made her feel closer to him.

She gave Jake his exclusive interview, which was more about Dalton than about her. She asked him to send it to print the day before the concert. If people were going to talk about him, she wanted them to know the truth. Jake had found Bethany Waters and interviewed her as well. She told the world her story about the man who saved her life.

Samantha asked Jake to send a copy directly to Dalton because at the end of the interview when Jake asked her if she had any regrets, she told him yes. Her biggest regret was abusing herself. By leaving Dalton, she'd eviscerated her heart and soul. The longer she was separated from him, the more battered she felt. She'd given him her heart and left it behind. The last line of the story said, "I gave away my heart to the most deserving of men. I abandoned him in the most cowardly way. I only hope that he'll forgive me and tell me to come home."

Ray asked where home was for Samantha White, and she pressed her hand over her heart. The place where she'd tattooed his name. "Home is where Dalton is."

"Indigo, you're on in five," Oliver Shepherd called from the door of her dressing room. They'd had several meetings concerning their future together. He'd released her from her last album, hoping to sign her for three more. He wasn't the enemy. She'd been her own enemy. She'd allowed her fears to paralyze her. She'd allowed Dave to take over because it was easier. One thing she learned along the way was, easy wasn't always best. Some things were worth fighting for.

Freedom.

Family.

The truth.

Her reputation.

Friendship.

Change.

Love.

Those were the things worth battling for. The hardest fight should always be for love.

Samantha looked down at her cast. In faded silver letters, she saw Dalton's inscription. "It's all about love."

Yes, it is. She put on her headset and made her way to the side of the stage. Deanna stood by with a bottle of water.

"Everything you want is out there."

Samantha gave her a weak smile. "Not everything."

Deanna gave her a push. "Yes. Everything," she said and winked.

The only thing Samantha wanted was a second chance. She put on her game face and rushed out to please the crowd. "Hello, Los Angeles!" Her voice didn't reveal her brokenness. Dave had been right about one thing. The fans looked to her for hope and inspiration. She'd give it to them.

She looked into the crowd of thousands and wondered how many of them had ever felt a love as profound as she felt for Dalton. "I'm so happy to be here tonight."

She looked at the signs people held that said, "I love you."

"I love you, too, but I want to start off by saying that you have to love yourself first. Allow yourself to be loved. Many of you are the victims of abuse. Love doesn't come easy, but open your hearts because love is worth it."

She walked to the edge of the stage and shook a few hands. The band played one of the songs she wrote while in Aspen Cove. "This is a song I wrote for a very special man. I want Dalton Black to know that I love him. It's called 'One Hundred Wishes'. My wishes begin and end with him." She took a deep breath. Saying his name made her heart race. "A woman told me that wishes cost nothing; that thoughts were important. Let's hear everyone scream out a wish." She held out her microphone while the crowd screamed their wishes.

Her headset crackled and hissed. She adjusted the volume, hoping the interference would disappear. She tapped on the earpiece, but it didn't help. In a low voice she recognized, she heard, "My wish is for you to come home. Come home to me." It played over and over and over until it was no longer in her headset but echoing through the stadium. The electronic displays flashed the words *come home, come home, come home to me.*

Confused, she turned to stage left where she'd left Deanna and found she was no longer there. She turned to stage right, which was also empty. The beat of the song got louder. Dalton's voice was modulated to fill in the backbeat. She moved to center stage, confused. She lifted the microphone to sing. The crowd parted, and up the steps walked Dalton Black, dressed to kill. He was a man of simple tastes, but he made jeans and a black T-shirt look better than an Armani suit.

Samantha stopped dead still. She blinked several times to make sure he was there. The crowd went wild. Many held signs that read, "Dalton is my hero." Her heart nearly seized.

"See ... wishes do come true." She threw herself into his arms. After he twirled her around and kissed her stupid, he set her down. "You've got a concert to perform."

She looked into his blue eyes. How she ever thought they looked like cold steel, she didn't know. They were filled with molten blue love. "Don't leave me."

He shook his head. "Never."

"What happens next?" Afraid that he'd disappear, she didn't want to let him go.

"I'm taking you home."

"You're here. I'm home already."

For the next hour and fifty-two minutes, Samantha sang about love and hope, and she believed every word that came out of her mouth because clarity wasn't always found in the messiness of life. It was found in the eyes of love.

CHAPTER THIRTY-ONE

Samantha had been back in Aspen Cove for a week, but no one would have known it because she and Dalton barely left the bed. They got up only to shower, eat, and binge-watch *Supernatural*.

"You're really buying the paper mill?" Dalton's hand rubbed her bare stomach, which was no longer concave. His skills in the kitchen came second only to his skills in the bedroom. His fingers trailed up her stomach to her chest, where she'd tattooed the word 'Dalton's' over her heart.

"Yes, I'm investing in some much-needed improvements here in Aspen Cove."

"What are you going to do here?"

She rolled her naked body on top of him. She knew he wouldn't have much to say because he couldn't think when they were naked.

"I'm building a recording studio. It's a bit selfish, but I never want to leave home again."

"Sometimes we have to be selfish." Several times, their friends had come to the door to say hello and Dalton growled at them that he wasn't ready to share her, but tonight was karaoke night, and he had no choice. "What else is going in the paper mill?"

She ran her hands down his chest. Goosebumps rose beneath her fingertips. "It will be the Guild Creative Center. I want it to be a place where artistic people can thrive. Wes is putting put a culinary center next to a recording studio because I like to eat. I hope this sexy chef I know will be willing to work there on the days he's not working at Maisey's. I'm thinking maybe you can sell ready-made meals. You know, like take-and-bake. That would be a community service. No one would have to eat Sage's frozen lasagna again."

Dalton laughed. "I think we can negotiate on that."

"Now you want to negotiate?" She leaned down and bit his lip.

"No, right now I want to make love to my girlfriend. Who will be my fiancée, and then my wife, and the mother of my perfect children."

"Confident, are you?" She felt his confidence firm and long between her thighs.

"Would you have me any other way?" He lifted her hips and set her on top of him.

"I'll have you any way I can get you." She loved the way his eyes rolled back when she sank onto his length. The way he moaned her name when she rocked against him. The way loved flowed through his kisses.

"I'm all yours, baby." Dalton turned them over so he was on top. He found the perfect rhythm that made her body sing. How lucky was she to make love to a man who proved to be as yummy on the inside as he looked on the outside?

They made love right up until they had to shower and leave.

At six o'clock, they were the first to arrive for karaoke night. Cannon and Sage stood behind the bar.

"Did you come up for air?" Cannon asked.

"No, we came up for wine." Dalton slid onto a barstool and pulled Samantha into his lap.

"Are you hungry?" Sage wore a smile. In her hands were a spatula and a pan of frozen lasagna.

"No!" they said together.

"You're being mean. It's perfectly fine lasagna."

Everyone including Cannon shook their heads.

Next came Doc, followed by a white-haired woman everyone greeted as Agatha. Samantha's heart broke when Doc turned and she saw the oxygen tank and tubes. He wouldn't be singing "Hound Dog" tonight.

Dalton wrapped his arms around her. "Not your fault. No one blames you."

The door opened, and in walked Bobby and Louise Williams. She proudly displayed her baby bump and walked straight for Samantha.

"Thank you."

Samantha sucked in a big breath.

"For what?"

"I know you thought what happened was a bad thing. It wasn't a good thing, but it wasn't your fault. I'm thanking you because I got to have Bobby home for several weeks. We claimed some quality time together. It was like when we dated. When he was my boyfriend and I was his girlfriend."

"Doc has a girlfriend," Sage sang.

"Come here, you." Doc flagged her over. As soon as she got within range, he cuffed her lightly on the side of the head. "Get my Agatha a glass of wine. I'll have a cup of joe. Tell me again when that sister of yours is coming to take over? Louise is bound to have her last baby before then if she doesn't hurry."

Samantha looked to Dalton. "Doc and Agatha?"

He shrugged. "I told you love was like a virus. I got it. You caught it, and Doc caught it. Never too old to give love a chance."

A lot had happened while she was gone. "Lydia is coming?" she asked.

"That's the rumor, but that's all it is until she shows up." Dalton caught the pint of beer Cannon slid down the bar.

Next in the door were Katie and Bowie. Katie ran up to Samantha. "Did Daddy's jet work out okay?"

Samantha blushed. They had the plane to themselves and hit the mile high club twice on the short trip home. "It was amazing." She turned to Dalton. "Do you think we should get a plane like that?"

His eyes grew wide. "Can you afford a plane like that?"

She could see the list of possibilities running through his imagination.

"Probably."

Dalton tucked her close to his body and set his chin on top of her head. "No ... but maybe we can get a dock and a Jet Ski."

She picked up the glass of wine Cannon had poured her and smiled over the rim. "You're cheap," she told him.

"I may be cheap, but I'm not easy."

She made a *pfft* sound and rolled her eyes. "You are *so* easy." She turned in his lap and kissed him. Her voice softened. "Easy to love."

Katie kicked off karaoke night with another oldie but goodie. When she finished, she brought the mic to Samantha, who was happy to get up and sing for her friends, but Dalton took it and walked her to the stage. He set her on a stool in the center and looked into her eyes.

"This is a onetime deal. I'd hate to subject the town to this more than once in a lifetime." He picked his music and turned to Samantha. "This is for you." When he sang 'Amazed' by Lonestar, she nearly fell off her seat. Though Dalton's cooking skills and bedroom skills outshined his singing skills, the song was pitch-perfect because he sang to the deepest part of her heart. The part that belonged only to him.

When he finished, she was more in love with him than she thought possible.

When Samantha had walked off that stage in Denver months ago, there were three things she wanted more than money.

She wanted a life.

She wanted to love.

She wanted the freedom that came with being invisible.

Aspen Cove gave her life.

Dalton gave her love.

And Samantha realized she'd never be invisible. Not to her fans. Not to her friends. Not to the one man who hadn't known her and saw who she was anyway.

As she looked around Bishop's Brewhouse, she knew without a doubt she was home.

THANK YOU FOR READING.

Do you love talking books with other readers?

Join Kelly Collins' Book Nook for prizes, books, and live chats.

Kelly Collins' Book Nook

Want to be the first to know about new releases?

Sign up here for members-only exclusives, including advance notice of pre-orders, as well as contests, giveaways, freebies, and special deals.

You can also follow me on Bookbub

NEED MORE ASPEN COVE?

An Aspen Cove Romance Series

One Hundred Reasons

One Hundred Heartbeats

One Hundred Wishes

One Hundred Promises

One Hundred Excuses

One Hundred Christmas Kisses

To see more Kelly Collins' Books Click Here

ACKNOWLEDGMENTS

I started out with book one of the Aspen Cove Series with the goal of writing a heartwarming small town romance. I had a series in mind but didn't know if readers would love my small town full of quirky people.

Boy was I glad you do because I love writing about this town.

None of this would be as good without an editor. Thanks to Karen Boston for her work on this manuscript.

Thanks to the ladies who proofread this book. Judy, Sabrina, Melissa and Tammy, what would I do without your keen eyes?

Thank you to Victoria Cooper for the amazing cover which is photographed by Darren Birks of Darren Birks Photography. He made the perfect Dalton and Catherine made the perfect Samantha.

Last but never least, I thank you the reader for being loyal fans. I hope you enjoy your time in Aspen Cove. There's so much more to come.

GET A FREE BOOK.

Go to www.authorkellycollins.com

ABOUT THE AUTHOR

International bestselling author of more than thirty novels, Kelly Collins writes with the intention of keeping the love alive. Always a romantic, she blends real-life events with her vivid imagination to create characters and stories that lovers of contemporary romance, new adult, and romantic suspense will return to again and again.

Kelly lives in Colorado at the base of the Rocky Mountains with her husband of twenty-seven years, their two dogs, and a bird that hates her. She has three amazing children, whom she loves to pieces.

For More Information
www.authorkellycollins.com
kelly@authorkellycollins.com

Made in the USA
Middletown, DE
25 November 2020